THE MERMAID'S SISTER

CARRIE · ANNE · NOBLE

SKYSCAPE

SKYSCAPE

Published by Skyscape, New York

www.apub.com

Amazon, the Amazon logo, and Skyscape are trademarks of Amazon.com, Inc., or its affiliates.

ISBN-13: 9781477820889
ISBN-10: 1477820884

Cover design by M.S. Corley

Library of Congress Control Number: 2014912866

Printed in the United States of America

For my sister Kate—
safe in the arms of her true Father
but missed every day.

CHAPTER ONE

Llanfair Mountain, Pennsylvania
1870

Wishing gets you nothing.

These words are old wounds carved into the trunk of an ancient tree. Above the vandal's warning, the tree stretches evergreen limbs across the glassy-surfaced Wishing Pool. Below, its dark roots twist and trail into the water.

Do trees make wishes? I do not think so.

But I am wishing.

I wish that my sister would come out of the water. I can see her resting on the perfect, round pebbles at the bottom of the pool, the ones tossed in by visitors over hundreds of years, the ones said to be required by the pool sprite as payment. *One perfect pebble for each wish.* Such pebbles are rare in the world—as rare as magic itself.

Bubbles rise from Maren's mouth, each one slowly drifting to the surface before popping. Her eyes are closed, her body is as still as a corpse. Little gray fishes nibble at the fabric of her floating petticoat. As she dreams, her webbed toes twitch and a smile spreads across her face.

She never looks so happy on the land.

"Come out," I say, knowing she will not—even if she does hear me. She never obeys me.

Behind me, twigs crack and leaves rustle. I turn to see our wyvern lifting one foot and then the other, fussing at the moss and sticks between his birdlike toes. His blue scales, pale as a summer sky on his belly and dark as midnight on his back, catch the dim light like curved slices of stained glass. He nods his dragonny head and snorts. Auntie has sent him to bring us home for supper, no doubt.

"Good luck, Osbert darling," I say. "She's only been in for an hour."

Osbert spreads his wings wide and dives nosefirst into the pool with barely a splash. When he reappears, he brings Maren with him, his sharp teeth clutching the back of her camisole, like an enormous mother dog carrying a naughty puppy by the nape of its neck. When he releases her, she crumples onto the muddy shore. Osbert tickles her neck with his barbed tail and snorts encouragement over her motionless body.

Finally, she awakens with a gasp, sits up, and swats at the watchful wyvern. "Go home, you beast!"

Osbert's ears flatten and he skulks away, whining.

"He thinks he saved your life," I say. "You could be kinder to him."

She does not speak again until we are halfway home, at the place where the forest and meadow meet. She plucks a cornflower from its stalk and says quietly, "Someday I will stay in the water. Someday I won't come out."

My heart sinks, down, down. I can think of no reply.

She tosses the flower away and says, "Will you visit me, Clara, when I live in the sea with my mermaid sisters? Will you come in a boat and bring me cherries from Auntie's tree? Will you come and sing our songs? Will you bring O'Neill?"

"What about Osbert?"

"You may leave the silly wyvern at home. But you must promise to come." She reaches for my hand. Her webbed fingers are still dripping with Wishing Pool water.

They are more webbed than they were last summer.

I stare at them, my sister's strange fingers. Until our sixteenth birthday, she had hands like mine. Same size, same shape, same chipped nails stained with tree sap or mud, ink or dyes. Twin hands, although we are not of the same blood. But now, her hands are changing.

She is changing.

I am losing her. I wish I would not.

But wishing gets you nothing.

With a long match, Auntie lights the three fat, yellow candles in the center of the oaken kitchen table. The scent of beeswax mingles with the scents of vegetable stew and fresh bread. She waves the match in the air like a magic wand and its flame transforms into a puff of white smoke. The smoke curls and stretches into a halo around Auntie's gray hair.

"Come and sit here, Maren," Auntie says.

Arms crossed, Maren plods to the chair. She tosses her head and her honey-colored curls bounce about her slim shoulders. She casts a scowl my way to let me know that she knows I told on her.

Auntie takes Maren's pale hands in her plump, wrinkled ones, turns them this way and that, then holds them close to the candles. And she sighs.

"Now I know why you've taken to wearing gloves of late," Auntie says.

Maren's cheeks redden and she stares at the tablecloth.

"I should have expected the change to come quickly once you turned sixteen. I hope you will forgive an old woman for not being a better mother. For not better preparing you for what's to come. Now, is there anything else you should show me, Maren?" Auntie asks, releasing her hands. She lifts Maren's chin so that she must meet her gaze. "The truth, my dear."

A few seconds pass before Maren pulls her bodice away from the waistband of her skirt. She clutches the fabric so that her side is exposed.

"My, my," Auntie mutters.

Beneath a layer of alabaster skin I see rows of pale-green scales, starting just at the dainty curve of Maren's waist. Delicate scales, small and silver-edged.

I am on my feet before I know it. I reach out and touch my sister's side, feeling the ridges. They are real, not a trick of the light as I'd hoped. I have kept my worries about Maren to myself for too long.

"Auntie?" I whisper. "Can you cure her? Should I fetch the remedy book?" Auntie is famous among the folk of the mountain for the medicines she concocts from our herb gardens and the bounty of the forest.

"No, child." Auntie's voice is gentle but firm. "You know I cannot. There is no cure for being who you truly are."

"But, Auntie . . ." I cannot find words to form the hundred questions swirling in my head, my heart.

"We've been pretending," Auntie says. "Pretending that your sister's transformation was something yet to come, instead of something that has always been happening, bit by bit. But you can't erase a thing by not acknowledging it."

Auntie places one hand on Maren's shoulder and the other on mine. "Your lives are wonders, my girls. They will be wonders from start to finish. Do you not remember the story of how you came to me?"

"The seashell and the stork. You tell us every birthday," Maren volunteers. Her smile is sweet and strange at the same time. Beautiful and eerie.

"And can I lie?" Auntie asks.

"Never," Maren and I say in unison, knowing Auntie's part-faerie blood keeps her from speaking falsely.

Auntie smoothes her flowered apron before perching her ample bottom on her favorite wooden stool. "Shall I tell you again?"

"Oh, yes!" Maren says, her eyes sparkling with delight.

I nod. Perhaps, if I pay close attention to the story, the weight of my dread over Maren's condition will lessen—at least for a little while.

Placing her folded hands in her lap, Auntie begins.

"It was October, of course. Both of you came to me in October. The winds were fierce one night, rattling the windows and howling down the chimney like unhappy ghosts. Rain pelted the roof like rocks thrown by a family of giants. Osbert was in a state, moaning and pacing in front of the parlor fireplace. He kept tripping over my knitting basket and getting tangled in my good wool yarn. I was just about to banish him to the cellar when a knocking started at the kitchen door. I left Osbert in his tangle—a good place for him, as it kept him restrained so he couldn't scare the visitor. But when I opened the door, not a soul was there. 'Yoo-hoo!' I called. 'You're welcome to come in for a cup of tea! Nasty night this is!' But no one answered. I was just about to shut the door when it caught my eye: a great conch shell just lying there on the path like the tide had gone out without it. Never mind that no tide ever touches Llanfair Mountain. That seashell was as big as my good soup pot. I'd never seen the like! Being partial to seashells, I brought it inside and set it on this very table to admire it. It was wet with rain, so I used the hem of my apron to polish it dry. And when I tipped it, a tiny bundle rolled out onto the table—a little blanket woven of seaweed with the smallest face I'd ever seen peeking out. Here was a babe just as pink and white as the inside of the conch. She wore a little scallop shell on her head as a bonnet. That child was you, Maren."

"I came from the sea, and to the sea I must return," Maren says, as nonchalantly as one might say, "Two plus two equals four."

"Indeed," Auntie says. "Did I ever tell you otherwise?"

"Never," Maren says, looking quite pleased. "Now, tell us about Clara." Maren pours tea into her mug and adds two teaspoons of salt, as is her habit. No one craves salt like our Maren.

"Well, it wasn't but three days later. I'd just put Maren in her cradle for a nap. I went to the window to check the weather because I'd hung my best quilt out to air and the red-sky morning had promised rain. That's when I saw *him*. I stood stock-still, and I watched him come closer and closer. The clouds slid a thick veil over the sun, and in the dimness his eyes shone like two bits of polished coal. He was carrying a cloth-covered bundle like it was the most precious thing in the world. I ran out to meet him, and he placed the gift in my arms."

"Beware of storks bearing gifts," Maren says, poking me. I slap her arm in reply.

Auntie chuckles. "Let me finish, girls! As I was saying, I took that bundle in my arms, and folded back the edge of the cloth to find another wee babe. Fast asleep you were, your black lashes lying against your cheeks like miniature raven's wings. 'A sister for Maren,' I said. When I looked up to thank him, he was gone."

"Who? Who was the one who brought me?" I am desperate for a comforting answer. "Was it my true father?" She has never said so before, but perhaps today she might tell me more.

"No, not your father, dear. A stork brought you, Clara mine. You know this. The most beautiful stork I'd ever seen."

Raised with just enough magic to unquestioningly assume that someday I would become a stork, I had never before found the story particularly disturbing. But on this day, with the evidence of Maren's transformation before my eyes and beneath my fingertips, I give way to panic. Trembling, I ask what I have not until now. "Auntie, are you saying that one day I'll sprout wings like Maren is sprouting scales?"

"I said nothing of the kind, Clara my dear." Auntie lovingly caresses the top of my head. "You worry too much. Worrying gets you nothing."

"Like wishing," I say. I slump in my chair and close my eyes.

"What *I* wish right now is that someone would see to the hens," Auntie says. The discussion is clearly over. "Go on, Clara—and you may fetch some firewood, Maren."

"Yes, Auntie," we say together, like twins. We catch one another's eyes. In Maren's, I can see the green-blue of the ocean. A tide of sorrow rushes over my heart.

The ocean is so very far away.

How will I live without my sister? She is the strong one, the outgoing one, the shiny-as-a-new-coin one. The one the village boys smile at, the one who charms extra pennies from the shrewdest of housewives when we sell our vegetables in the square.

What am *I* without her?

Just a girl left by a stork.

CHAPTER TWO

Osbert races back and forth in front of the cottage, shrieking and galloping like a crazed, two-legged miniature pony. His unruly pointed tail knocks the heads off the black-eyed Susans and tears up the grass by its roots.

"Osbert, hush," I say. "Go inside, you beast!" I do not know what has provoked him to act so wildly. It could be anything from a trespassing chipmunk to an approaching villager. And if it is the latter, he would do well to hide himself. Few people believe dragons still exist—especially not the practical folk of Llanfair Mountain. It is better for us all if his presence remains a secret.

When I hear the clanging, I know why Osbert is in such a state. Scarff and O'Neill are coming, and Osbert loves no one better, not even Auntie, who raised him from an egg.

Pots and pans bump and bang together as they swing from hooks under the eaves of the brightly painted house-wagon, above the sign that reads "Scarff and Brady, Merchants." Funny wind chimes made of old spoons and knives, chimes crafted from bits of pottery and sea glass, and chimes created from pieces of copper pipe and tin soldiers add their notes to the music of the caravan's approach. This symphony lifts my heart like no other, for it means the arrival of beloved friends.

Auntie steps out of the cottage, a wide smile on her round face. The unmistakable smile of a woman in love. For as old as they might be now, my dear Auntie Verity and Ezra Scarff have been sweethearts (according to Auntie) since her hair was chestnut-brown and his beard was the color of dandelions.

From his seat behind his faithful horses, Job and January, Scarff waves with both hands. Before the caravan stops, a young man leaps out its back door, turns a somersault in the air, and lands squarely on two green-shoed feet.

"O'Neill!" Maren shouts, in a most unladylike fashion, from across the garden. To reinforce her lack of manners, she runs to him and embraces him with such vigor that they both stumble and fall into the dusty road.

I blush in embarrassment for my sister. She would not consider being embarrassed for herself.

And then I pick up my skirts and hurry to meet O'Neill. "You've grown taller," I say as he regains his footing and brushes the dirt from his tan trousers and brightly embroidered vest.

"Scarff tells me that he absolutely will not buy me another pair of trousers till next spring, even if they're at my knees come New Year's Day," the blond young man says, laughing. He embraces me before I can object. Not that I would have, truly. He smells of spices and strong soap, like Christmas morning come early. "There now," he says. "Now I am made welcome."

Osbert leaps the garden gate and tackles O'Neill, licking his face with a forked and silvery tongue.

"Ha!" Maren says. "*Now* you are made welcome, indeed!" She puts a hand over her mouth and giggles. The webbing between her fingers extends almost to her knuckles, a pale, translucent green.

"Osbert! Get off me, you behemoth!" O'Neill does not laugh with Maren. His eyes are fixed on her affected hand.

Noticing, Maren slips her hands into the pockets of her skirt. "What are you staring at, peddler boy?" Her teasing is accompanied by the batting of eyelashes, a blatant attempt to distract O'Neill from what he has seen.

With a scowl, O'Neill pushes Osbert aside—and it is no small feat to move an agitated hundred-pound wyvern. He stands up, filthy and frowning. "Show me your hands, Maren."

"No." Her lower lip protrudes in an unusually charming pout.

He grabs at her arm and tries to pull her hand from its hiding place. She lets out a shriek.

"What is all this?" a voice booms, silencing everything, right down to the last bird in the hedges. Scarff approaches like a slow-moving thundercloud, his typically jolly expression absent from his bushy-bearded face. "O'Neill! Have I brought you up to accost young ladies and thereby cause them to rent the air with tones befitting a tribe of banshees?"

"Not at all, sir." O'Neill steps away from Maren and stands as straight and solemn as a soldier.

Scarff taps O'Neill's elbow with his ebony walking stick. "What have you to say to the lady?"

"I beg your pardon, Maren," O'Neill says crisply.

"Now, boy, since you are remembering your manners, perhaps you could show the ladies our recent acquisitions. The Turkish collection would certainly spark their interest." Finally, a smile blooms between Scarff's fluffy mustache and beard. "How we have missed you, dearest girls!" He lays a hand on one of my cheeks and one of Maren's and sighs like a king over his treasure hoard. "In all my days, in all this wide world, never have I seen such lovely girls. Except for one."

"Auntie Verity," Maren volunteers.

"Intelligent as well as beautiful, so you are." His laugh is a low rumble.

"Enough of your blather," Auntie says from behind her beau. "Come now, Ezra, and have tea with me while the children look at the wares."

He bows to us. "Your most humble servant." Arm in arm, Scarff and Auntie walk toward the cottage, their footsteps perfectly aligned.

"Come," O'Neill says.

All of our troubles and disputes vanish as we enter the caravan.

"Be lit," O'Neill commands as he turns the brass knob on the lantern suspended in the center of the room. An intense golden light floods every corner. I squint until the light fades to a more comfortable glow.

The caravan is magnificent. From hooks and pegs hang glass beads and strings of pearls, pendants of gold and enamelwork, chains of silver, and belts of leather as soft as a kitten's belly. Spoons carved from wood, plain and sturdy. Fishing lures and lutes, lamps and baskets. Dazzling ornaments and common kitchen knives. Shelves of bottled spices and stoppered glass vials (filled by Auntie and me last spring) holding curatives. At the far end, the curtained bed stands in tapestried glory, its fat feather mattress covered with a crazy quilt of velvet and silks.

As always, O'Neill mocks our wide-eyed amazement. To him, it is simply home and work. To us, it is beautiful and wild and exciting.

"Here," he says, pulling a richly lacquered chest out from beneath the sumptuous bed. He turns a key and the lid springs open. "We met a prince of the Ottoman Empire last month. He had been visiting a cousin in Philadelphia. He fell in love with the cousin's kitchen girl. He said she had eyes like stars and skin as fair as goat's milk. He sold us everything he'd brought from his faraway palaces so that he could buy her a little house beside the sea. His soul, he said, belonged to his bride, and he needed no other treasure but her."

"Oh! How romantic!" Maren declares.

"Wait until she loses her looks and her cheer after bearing him a dozen rowdy sons. How romantic that will be, sister," I say.

Maren and I sit on the Persian-carpeted floor and await O'Neill's presentation. For he is a natural showman, and relishes any opportunity to perform.

He peers into the trunk with a devilish grin, humming what must be a Turkish melody, slowly rifling through the contents. Suddenly, with a flourish, he presents us with a pair of pointy-toed, yellow silk slippers. "Behold! The shoes of Prince Asil, great prince of Anatolia, skilled in music, hunting, and the wooing of ladies both dark and fair! Note the rubies on the toes."

"Lovely," Maren says, taking one of the shoes from him. She removes a leather slipper and slips her foot into the prince's shoe. "What do you think?"

"They match your eyes, my lady," O'Neill says roguishly.

Maren smacks his arm. "You'll have yellow eyes if you do not mind yourself. Yellow, purple, black, and blue!"

One by one, O'Neill presents the prince's treasures. He sets them on the floor around us. We marvel at the copper coffee set, the bejeweled dagger, the brass candleholders, the embroidered robes, the jewelry box with the tiny silver turtle inside.

"Anatolia. I will never see such a place," Maren says. There is no regret in her words.

"I will take you to Anatolia," O'Neill says, "when we are twenty and no one can tell us what to do or where to go. I will take you both. We will see London and Paris. We will camp in deserts and on mountaintops, and float upon the Dead Sea waters. We will ride elephants and camels and eat strange dishes and drink strange wines. I will douse you in the perfumes of the Orient, and cover you with silken saris, and pierce your noses with diamonds, and pierce your ears with pearls."

Maren and I exchange a look.

"Keeping secrets, are you?" O'Neill asks. "From your best friend in the world? Your almost-brother?"

Biting her lip, Maren removes one royal shoe and stretches her foot toward O'Neill. "See for yourself." She fans her odd toes, showing webbing that belongs on the foot of a frog, not the foot of a young lady.

He grabs her foot. "It is nothing," he says. "I have seen worse things cured. I once saw a pig-headed man transformed into an ordinary banker. And on a Tuesday, no less."

"It is far too warm in here," Maren says. She removes her other shoe and pelts O'Neill in the chest with it. "Last one to the Wishing Pool is a slimy newt!"

In the moment before we chase after Maren, O'Neill grabs my hand. "I will see that she is cured," he vows. "Trust me, Clara."

And then we are running through the forest, and once again I am wishing. Wishing that I could trust in O'Neill's promise. Wishing that he could be the hero of the story of Maren's life, as he was once the hero of our games of make-believe.

Chapter Three

The bonfire blazes. The visiting village children dance around it, their small feet kicking and stepping to the music of Auntie's violin. Their parents sit on blankets nearby, or stand beside the long trestle tables, sampling peculiar pastries and miniature star-shaped cakes. An hour ago, Scarff and O'Neill set the tables themselves with brocaded cloths, silver candlesticks, and box after box of sweets and savories pulled from the depths of the caravan.

I slip a mysterious pastry into my mouth, wondering about its origin. Wondering if it will be stale and I will have to swallow it for good manners' sake. I wondered for nothing. It is delicious. Despite the warmth of the summer evening, each bite cools the palate like snow while pleasing the tongue with curious flavors: lemon and sage, honey and black pepper.

My heart is light and heavy at the same time. Light because of the music and the ninety-nine sparkling lanterns hanging from posts and tree branches, and the laughter of my sister as old Mr. Fig whirls her about. Heavy because tomorrow morning Scarff and O'Neill will hitch Job and January to the wagon and leave our mountain. Heavy because for all of O'Neill's paging through books, he has found no remedy for Maren . . . and I know he will not, for I have spent many long nights searching those same tomes while Auntie and Maren slept.

O'Neill pulls me to my feet. "Worry-bird," he teases, "do you not trust me to do as I have sworn?"

In his arms, my heart races. His spicy Christmas scent, the sparkle of his blue eyes—things that have always given me familial comfort—are suddenly unsettling and unfamiliar. Is it the magic of the setting, I wonder, or something else? All I know is that I cannot move and do not want to.

But then he tugs me toward the dancers. "Nothing like a jig to chase one's cares away," he says with a wink.

I stumble along behind him. "Spoken like a true Irishman."

"Or a German, a Frenchman, an Italian, or a Swede." He laughs. "Whatever I may be."

And then we are dancing. To me, the dance is as magical as one of O'Neill's hat tricks, for it makes joy appear out of thin air.

When the moon is over the apple orchard, a flash of lightning and a rumble of thunder send the villagers scurrying home.

"Wasn't that convenient?" I say to O'Neill as he plops to the ground between Maren and me. The firelight reveals his impish grin.

"Am I to blame that your mountain folk do not care for my fireworks? I try so hard to entertain, but alas! Not everyone appreciates my art."

Maren lays her head on his shoulder, her unbraided hair spilling down his shirtfront like a many-tiered waterfall. "You, O'Neill, are a mischief," she says fondly.

The look he gives her is full of tenderness. An arrow of jealousy pierces my chest.

"What have we here?" booms Scarff as he and Auntie approach arm in arm. "A rare set of conjoined triplets?" His laughter echoes through the cooling night air, rebounds off the bumpy surface of the moon.

Scarff unfolds two wooden chairs he'd been carrying under his arm. He and Auntie settle into them, their shoulders touching, their wrinkled fingers entwined.

"Tell us the story," Maren says. "Of how we were almost triplets. Please?"

"Again?" moans O'Neill. "Must we hear it every time Scarff and I come to visit?"

"Hush, now," Auntie says. "I know for a fact that we have not heard the tale for three years now. And it is one of my favorites."

From the pocket of his pinstriped suit coat, Scarff retrieves his wooden pipe. The bowl is carved with the fierce face of a bear. It used to frighten me when I was small. From another pocket, he withdraws a black leather pouch of tobacco. In his habitual manner, Scarff dips the pipe into the pouch, uses two fingers to tamp the tobacco down, and then lights it with a flint. He takes his time, most likely to make Maren squirm.

She squirms. "It will be daylight before you manage to tell the story," she whines.

Scarff laughs. "Very well. I will begin." He blows three smoke rings and clears his throat.

Groaning, Maren throws herself back onto the grass.

"Well, Miss Impatient," Scarff scolds, "if you are going to take a nap, I will not waste my breath with storytelling."

Auntie pinches him hard enough to elicit an "Ouch!"

"Long, long ago," he begins, "when you girls were babes in arms, I drove the wagon up to the gates of a beautiful church. It was early November, and I was chilled clear to my bones. A cold snap had come up, you see, so although I was in the south, the weather was terribly disagreeable. The church stood tall against the gray skies like a castle of old. Billows of smoke floated up from the rectory's chimney, so I thought to myself that perhaps I could find warm refuge there. I had traded goods with priests before for shelter and a hot meal. So I tied my horses to the iron fence. Their names were Frederick and February. A fine pair of horses they were. Frederick was a bay and stood—"

"For goodness' sake!" Maren says with a huff. "Skip the horse part!"

Scarff chortles and blows more smoke rings, clearly relishing the hassle he is giving Maren. "So, where was I? Oh, yes, the churchyard. I walked in and headed for the rectory, skirting the gravestones out of respect. That's when I heard the most dreadful wailing. At first I thought I'd disturbed one of the residents of the graveyard, so unearthly was the sound. Despite my goose bumps, I followed the wailing around the side of the church and through a gate into what must have been a most magnificent garden in the spring or summer. Past the leafless rosebushes and blackberry patches, underneath the bare branches of one of the largest apple trees I have ever seen, there knelt a black-robed man. His back was to me, and he was hunched over, and the terrible sound was coming from him." Scarff leans back and shuts his eyes. "I can see it plain as day, that scene. I still dream of it almost every night."

Auntie smiles and pats his arm.

"I wondered if I should disturb the man. His grief was so raw, his cries so full of anguish. But I could not leave any creature alone to suffer so, neither man nor beast. 'Pardon me, Father,' I said. 'Can I help you somehow?' He turned toward me then, his face swollen with weeping, and held out his arms."

Maren grabs one of my hands and one of O'Neill's. Her face glows with excitement.

"There, in a willow basket, wrapped in a tangle of rags, lay a baby no bigger than the scrawniest of barn cats. Fast asleep, oblivious to the priest's carrying-on. 'Thanks be to God!' the priest shouted. 'Thanks to Our Lady and all the saints and angels on high!' Well, I took a step back. Thought he must be a lunatic—or too fond of the Communion wine or some such thing. 'You must take the child! It is the will of the Lord!' he said. I stepped back again. 'Father,' I said, 'I am afraid I do not comprehend your meaning.' The tears rolled down his face like rain down window glass. He said, 'My brother Seamus is buried beneath this apple tree. He died forty years ago today. That is why I came here this evening. And what did I find but this helpless babe, and him with the same heart-shaped birthmark on his chin as our Seamus had?'"

Scarff pauses so that all may turn to look at O'Neill's chin. O'Neill rolls his eyes, but he is smiling, too.

"'Take him,' the priest begged. 'I am too old for infants, and I would not send a half-dead dog to our county orphanage.' I could not speak, so aghast I was. Then the child opened his eyes and looked right through me. As if compelled by forces unseen, I opened my arms wide. The priest did not wait one second before shoving the basket into my grasp. Then he kissed my cheeks. 'Glory be to God,' he said, shaking like a leaf. 'Bless you, my son. Bless you through all the ages, forever and ever!' He smiled from ear to ear. He had but three teeth to his name, I swear. I watched him limp off to the church, and there I was, left holding a baby, of all things. I glanced at the marker in the roots of the apple tree. 'Seamus O'Neill,' it said. 'Rest in Peace.' I looked at the child and he looked at me. I said, 'Lad, you surely don't look like a Seamus to me. So O'Neill it shall be.' And he reached a little hand up and yanked my beard. Unfortunately, I fell in love with the creature then and there."

"Dear little baby O'Neill," Maren teases. "Sweet little beard tugger." O'Neill nudges her with his shoulder and she collapses in a fit of giggling.

Tapping his pipe upside down against the ground, Scarff continues. "Much as I loved the child, I did not think the life of a roving peddler suitable for him. So when spring came, I traveled to Pennsylvania with a mission. I planned to give him to Verity as a brother for the two girls she'd adopted. He'd have a good home, good food, lots of love, and woods to roam. But O'Neill had other plans. Turns out he was the only baby ever to dislike Verity Amsell in the history of mankind!"

"Go on!" Auntie says, laughing. "He liked me fine. But the boy knew his place, and his place was with you. He cried so loudly every time you left the room that I knew I'd be deaf in a day if you left him with me."

"So it was. O'Neill chose me and a traveler's life. And, truly, I would not have had it any other way," Scarff says with a wistful grin and a fat tear in the corner of his eye.

"He did not want two sisters. That is why he howled so," I offer.

"True enough," O'Neill says. "Who could stand having to live in the same house with girls like you?"

I wish you'd stay forever, I think.

I wish that I would not wish so often.

Chapter Four

In the morning, Scarff and O'Neill are gone.

It is how they always leave, quietly, without good-byes. Without tears or promises to return on a certain day or in a certain month.

They will come back before they go south for the winter, I am sure.

Before breakfast, when I rise alone to feed the chickens, I find a folded scrap of paper in my boot beside the door. "Remember my promise and fret not," it says. It is signed with a fancy O so full of swirls it reminds me of a tornado. I press the paper to my heart as if it were a love letter.

Is it wrong to feel so happy about a simple note when my sister is on the brink of becoming half fish?

The hens scurry back and forth and cluck with excitement when they see me. I scatter corn for them and watch them peck and scratch. They are happy because their puny brains do not allow for what-ifs or guilt or wishing. But I do not wish to be a chicken any more than I wish to become a stork, because then I would not have a glorious bit of paper signed with a swirling O inside my pocket.

When I return to the cottage, Gretel Goodling is waiting for me on the doorstep, her cheeks rosy from her early-morning hike up the mountain. She shifts her weight from foot to foot with all the impatience one would expect from a thirteen-year-old girl sent on an errand.

"Is your brother ill again?" I ask.

"Yes. Another fever and cough," she says. "Mama wants me to ask Miss Verity to come down to him. He's that bad."

I lead Gretel inside and call for Auntie. While Auntie gathers her medicines, Gretel and I share a pot of tea.

"Have you heard about the traveling show?" Gretel asks. "Mama says they'll be selling unreliable medicines but that we can go for the music and such. It's tonight, in the Pinkneys' fallow field."

Maren enters the kitchen yawning and fastening the top button of her blouse with lace-gloved fingers. "Did you say something about a show?"

Gretel repeats the news, her enthusiasm increasing by the minute.

"We must go, too, Clara," Maren says, now wide awake and matching Gretel's excitement. "We never get shows here. Well, hardly ever. And don't say that O'Neill's antics count, because they do not."

"I am not interested in seeing silver-tongued salesmen and hearing bawdy songs sung by nearly undressed ladies," I say. "We can entertain ourselves at home in a more appropriate manner."

"Well, I'm going," Maren says. "Unchaperoned, if you will not come with me." She knows the word *unchaperoned* makes me cringe. "Auntie, please tell Clara that she must go see the traveling show with me tonight. I might never get another chance, after all."

"You should go with Maren, Clara." Auntie covers her basket of herbs and bottles with a clean towel. "Widen your horizons, dear. Dance with the village boys and enjoy your youth."

"There—it's settled," Maren says proudly. "And perhaps O'Neill would like to come. Where is he? Out seeing to his horses?"

"They've gone," I say. "In their usual way."

"Scarff doesn't care for a fuss," Auntie says. "So we won't pout over it, will we, my girls?"

Maren pouts.

"At least you have the show to look forward to, sister," I say, even though I am not looking forward to it one bit. I pour a cup of tea and set it before her. "And they will be back before you know it."

"True enough," Auntie says. She picks up her basket. "Come along now, Gretel, and we'll see what's to be done about your brother."

O'Neill's note crinkles inside my pocket as I cross the kitchen to refill the teapot, a secret treasure hidden among the folds of my everyday garment. If I must go to the show, I will carry it with me.

It is a more than adequate consolation.

A section of farmer Pinkney's field is marked off with flaming torches, each as tall as a man. Within this boundary, rows of benches face a raised stage. Above the stage, lanterns hang from a wire and cast a warm glow on the plank floor.

The villagers gather at the boundaries, seeming to hesitate, as if going any farther would be equivalent to entering a fairy circle or haunted place. Only a few young people venture to the benches. They are wearing their best clothes, and so is Maren—whether it's to impress one another or in honor of the rare event, I do not know.

Maren pulls me by the sleeve of my second-best dress until we reach the center of the third-row bench. Immediately, Simon Shumsky and Daniel Roberts take seats beside us. Daniel sits close enough to me that I can feel the warmth of his thigh through the fabric of my dress and petticoat. His breath makes no secret of the fact that he had onions for supper, washed down with beer. I slide closer to my sister and make use of my fan.

Simon flirts with Maren, and she flirts back. She is only playing, but he has asked her to marry him at least three times this year. He is neither very bright nor very handsome, but he *is* rich and determined. I wonder if she would have said yes to him someday—for all the wrong reasons—had she not been destined to become a mermaid.

The thought of Maren's future form sends a shiver of dread through my body. How long will she be able to remain with us on the mountain? And who will take her to the sea when the time comes? I could never be brave enough to take her there alone. I have heard far too many stories of perilous roads and dangerous strangers. And beyond that, how could I keep her safe and hidden? Perhaps with O'Neill's aid . . .

I stare at Maren's pretty profile and try to comfort myself with the truth: my sister is not afraid of becoming a mermaid. She has spoken of it since we were very young, and never with dismay. Quite the opposite, in fact. I think the romance of life in an underwater kingdom appeals to her greatly.

If I were more like her, I might relish the thought of the feathers and wings I will grow one day if or when I become a stork—instead of accepting my possible fate without joy, as I do now.

The music of a flute wafts over the crowd and distracts me from my woeful reverie. Finally, the villagers dare to step into the bounds of the show, finding seats and shushing noisy children and spouses. Near the back of the platform, a red velvet curtain parts, and a woman walks to center stage. Her skin is the color of caramel, and her small, lithe body is wrapped in a sunset of silks. Gold rings adorn her ears and a diamond sparkles on her nostril. She spreads her arms wide and begins to sing.

She sings in deeply accented English, a song about a caged bird's longing for freedom. Her voice soars and dips like a swallow in flight. Suddenly, or so it seems, the song is over. The audience applauds and cheers. Beside me, Daniel Roberts whistles—and then looks at me sheepishly and apologizes.

A short, stout, impeccably dressed gentleman takes the stage. He sweeps his top hat off his balding head and bows low. Then he says, "Ladies and gentlemen! I, Dr. George Wilhelm Hieronymus Lewis Balthazar Phipps, welcome you here tonight. You have just had the great privilege of hearing the beautiful songstress Madame Soraya of Gojanastani, the darling of the crowned heads of Europe and Asia. And now I present to you the handsome, the masterful, the celebrated Jasper Armand and his captivating violin!"

Dr. Phipps steps behind the curtain. He is replaced on the stage by a tall young man with a boyish face and a mop of brassy curls. He has the same eyes as the singer: golden-brown, like those of a mountain lion. He lifts the violin and, as promised, the audience is captivated.

Jasper plays with abandon, his face changing with each melody's mood. He moves from gentle lullaby to mournful ballad to rollicking jig. The jig brings the crowd to their feet and into the aisles. Simon and Maren twirl and canter and laugh. I am pulled and spun about by Daniel until I am quite dizzy.

"Take your seats, if you please," Dr. Phipps calls out when the music ends. "The great Jasper Armand shall entertain you again momentarily," he says. "First, I must deliver unto you a message of the greatest import. As a practitioner of the medical arts, I am bound by conscience to speak to you plainly, to reveal the deep secrets of healing I have gathered. Open your ears to the sound of my voice, ladies and gentlemen."

Dr. Phipps paces like a wildcat and extols like a preacher. "Have you aches and pains? Anxieties or doldrums? Skin rashes, stomach ailments, or digestive weakness? Have you women's problems? Coughs or colds? Wheezes or sneezes? Palsies or poxes? Poor memory or trouble sleeping? Would you like to feel young again? Behold, I bring you glad tidings! I, Dr. George Wilhelm Hieronymus Lewis Balthazar Phipps, possess the miracle you have been longing for. For every health issue you might be facing, I have developed an effective curative."

He pauses for a moment, using a bright-blue silk handkerchief to dab his damp brow. "How, you might ask, could one man find the cures for every sickness known to humankind? Well, my fine folks, I have consulted with physicians, scholars, shamans, wise men, wizards, scientists, and men of faith from across the globe. And the fruit of these studies is what I offer you here tonight: Dr. Phipps's Special Formulas. I offer you balms, elixirs, pills, and syrups—each suited for your specific affliction, and priced fairly so that I can help as many folks as possible." His expression of earnestness is every bit as theatrical as his speech.

He spreads his hands in a gesture of appeal. "Do not suffer another day, I beseech you. Visit the tables behind the stage after the show and purchase your new, healthy life tonight. We also offer fine soaps, tooth powders, painted fans, and gifts from far-away lands. Now, do not hesitate, my dear friends! Your miracle awaits you!"

I know he is a liar, for Auntie has warned us well of such men. But he is a skilled liar, and there is no way that I can stem the tide of customers rushing to buy his sham cures. As if to contrast the hectic movement, Jasper plays a mellow tune on guitar.

Simon takes Maren by the gloved hand. "I'll buy you something pretty, Miss Maren. Whatever you choose."

"That is very kind of you," she says. My sister is never one to refuse a gift.

I follow close behind Maren and Simon, losing Daniel in the throng. Every resident of the mountain (except Auntie) must be here tonight. And most of them seem extremely anxious to waste their money.

When we reach the tables, Maren points out a pair of embroidered silk gloves. Madame Soraya, now shop mistress, picks them up. "Try them. They will look beautiful with your ivory skin," she says. "Give me your hands and I will show you."

As quick as a striking snake, Madame Soraya takes hold of Maren's hands and pulls off her lace gloves. I gasp, and so does the show woman.

It is too late for my sister to hide her "affliction" from Madame Soraya. I look about, terrified that others might have seen. Auntie has kept our bits of magic (and our pet wyvern) secret all these years. She has warned us of the possible consequences of revealing our uniqueness: the loss of our home, our friends, and perhaps our lives.

To my relief, no one is staring at us. Even Simon seems not to have noticed Maren's hands. He stands half-turned away from the table, deep in conversation with the village mason.

Madame Soraya says, "I have seen this before. If you will meet me when the show is over, I will take you to Dr. Phipps. I am sure he can help you, child."

"It's nothing," Maren says, escaping Madame Soraya's grip and hiding her hands behind her back. "Just something that runs in my family, like freckles or large ears."

"You come and meet us," Madame Soraya insists. "It is a matter of life and death, child. You know this as well as I."

Maren turns away from the table. "I want to go home, Simon. They have nothing I want." Her pretty face is pale and her lower lip trembles.

"I will drive you home in my father's carriage," Simon says as he guides us through the crowd. "I could not call myself a gentleman if I allowed you girls to walk two miles up the mountain in the dark."

"Thank you, Simon," I say. "We appreciate your kindness."

Maren is uncharacteristically quiet during the ride home, no matter how hard Simon tries to amuse her. Poor Simon.

Later, safe at home in our shared bed, Maren says, "Perhaps you were right to want to stay home tonight. Perhaps I should try to be more sensible, like you."

I roll over to face her. "What fun would the world be if everyone was sensible like me?" I say. "What fun would I have if you allowed me to sit about reading all day? You make me live, sister. You keep me from being boring and bored."

"Thank you," she says. "Still, I would like to be better. Not always horrifying you and Auntie with my bad manners."

"Go to sleep, dear," I say, yawning. "You may reform in the morning—if you still wish to."

She is quiet for a moment, and then whispers, "I will stay home from now on, although I will most certainly hate it. I do not want to scare the boys with my scales and fins; I would rather remember them thinking me pretty." She rolls away from me and takes my share of the blankets with her. "Good night, Clara."

"Good night," I say.

Truth be told, I *do* wish we had stayed home. And I wish the medicine show woman had not caught a glimpse of Maren's webbed fingers. I hope Maren's careless revelation is quickly forgotten and does not bring consequences upon our little family.

My most fervent wish tonight, the last wish I will allow myself before surrendering to sleep, is for Madame Soraya and the dreadful medicine show to leave Llanfair Mountain before dawn and never return.

Chapter Five

August melts into September. Auntie and I harvest our crops of beans, potatoes, carrots, and beets. We gather herbs and hang them to dry in the attic. We pick grapes, pears, and apples. Every apple I pick reminds me of O'Neill, the apple tree child. I can no longer tell myself that I think of him only as my brother. I love him, and when he returns, I . . . I will most certainly *not* tell him.

Here on Llanfair Mountain (too many miles from wherever O'Neill may be), even the nosiest gossip fails to mention Maren's odd hands being revealed by the medicine show woman. For that, I am exceedingly grateful.

Maren is changing. Osbert follows her about, hanging his head and whimpering.

While Auntie and I work, Maren sits in the shallow end of the Wishing Pool if the weather is fine, or on a chair with her feet soaking in the washtub if there is a chill in the air. She must always be touching water now, as being completely dry causes her anxiety and discomfort.

She is losing her voice. Her loudest words come out as a whisper.

And the fishlike scales no longer hide beneath her skin's surface. Cool to the touch, they adorn her sides in silvery-green layers.

She hobbles on feet that are closer to fins.

When the pain of her body's transformation causes her to weep, tiny pearls fall from her eyes. She catches them in a bowl and buries them in the garden when she thinks Auntie and I are not looking. The garden is full of little mounds, as if an army of very industrious moles has taken up residence there.

I am glad we live two miles uphill from the village and rarely receive callers this time of year. But what if someone were to arrive and catch Maren unawares? She could not run to safety on her unwieldy fin-feet. She could not fight off even a salamander in her weakened state.

In a few weeks, Maren and I will be seventeen. I desire no gift more than the return of Scarff and O'Neill. Their presence would lift our spirits and distract Maren from her sufferings better than any medicine. And with any luck, O'Neill will bring some potion, pill, or enchantment to heal her, as he has sworn to do.

Day after day, I listen for the sound of clanging pots and pans and the music of Scarff's fantastic collection of wind chimes. I dream of it, and awake disappointed.

CHAPTER SIX

Christmas is next week. Auntie is stirring a pot of spiced apples on the wood-burning cookstove. The kitchen air is warm and when I breathe in, I can almost taste the cinnamon, cloves, and fruit. I knit clumsily, my stitches uneven and lumpy, while Maren dozes in the rocker at the hearthside. Her feet, which no longer look human at all, are soaking in a bucket of warm water. Bits of silver on her cheeks and brow catch the firelight. She looks beautiful and tragic, ill yet perfect.

Osbert bays like a hound and hurls himself into the cellar just before the pounding begins on the kitchen door. I throw a blanket over Maren, covering her from her neck to the floor as the visitor lets himself in, uninvited.

"A happy Christmas to you," says Simon Shumsky. He presses a wooden crate into Auntie's hands and then removes his hat. "Mother sent you a fruitcake, a jug of elderberry wine, and her greetings." His attention quickly turns to the shawl-covered girl. "Is she feeling poorly, Mrs. Amsell?"

Maren opens her eyes. "Oh, hello, Simon," she whispers.

"Well, thank you for stopping," I say. I grab his elbow and attempt to steer him toward the door, but he is built like an ox. And this ox is bent on getting closer to Maren.

"I am in no hurry to go, Miss Clara," he says, brushing past me.

Simon gets on one knee beside Maren, his square face inches from her sparkling cheekbone. "I came to ask you to the Christmas dance, Miss Maren. Father says I can use his new carriage. Your sister can come along, too. I bought a new suit last week just for the occasion." His adoring, eager smile makes me feel quite sorry for him.

"Too sick," Maren mutters. Her eyelids close.

"Well, you have eight days to get well. Doesn't your aunt have the cure for everything?" He places a small box in her blanket-covered lap. "I brought you a Christmas gift. I've been saving it for months."

Her eyelids flutter. "Thank you," she whispers.

"I am sorry, Simon," I say. "She simply cannot stay awake at times. It is her condition. I am sure she will enjoy opening your gift later."

He stands, still wearing the same lovesick face he always wears in Maren's presence. "I will pick her up for the dance on the twenty-sixth at three, Mrs. Amsell. And Clara, too, if she cares to go."

Auntie puts her hands on her hips. "We do thank you for your kind invitation, but Maren is too ill to go to the dance, Simon."

"Surely the sickness will pass," he says. "I will say many prayers, and I know you will nurse her well. If I may tell you a secret, I plan to announce our engagement at the dance."

"She has not agreed to marry you," I say. "She would have told us if she had."

Simon fingers the buttons of his woolen coat. "She has implied her consent. She likes to tease me, and that is why she pretends to refuse my offers. I know I can make her happy. I swear I will."

Auntie puts an arm about him and somehow maneuvers him to the door. "Good night, Simon. Thank your mother for the foodstuffs, will you?" Before he can don his hat, he is outside. Auntie shuts and locks the door.

"I've never seen a boy so smitten," Auntie says, turning back to the stove and stirring the preserves. "Perhaps I should brew up something to relieve him of that."

The box rolls off Maren's lap and I pick it up. "Can you do that?"

"Infatuation is easy to cure, if that is his problem. A little dandelion root, a sprig of hare-foot plant, a shaving of nutmeg, and a drop of moonrose nectar mixed into a cup of chamomile. True love is another story, I'm afraid. There is no cure for true love."

"I thought as much," I say. I turn the little box over in my hands and I think of my long-absent, much-missed friend O'Neill. I wonder if I could be cured of my feelings for him. It is not at all what I wish.

CHAPTER SEVEN

I recognize the thick, muffled feeling of snow in the air before I even open my eyes. I roll over to wish my sister a merry Christmas, but she is absent from the bed we have shared since we outgrew our extra wide cradle.

After slipping on woolen socks (hideously lumpy, made by me) and a robe of purple Chinese silk (last year's Christmas gift from O'Neill and Scarff), I hurry to the kitchen. The aroma of Auntie's special Christmas apricot scones meets me halfway.

With her fin-feet in a festively painted coal scuttle filled with water, Maren sits at the kitchen table. She has roses in her cheeks and a bright smile on her lips. The sash of her pink silk robe is tied in a huge bow.

"Merry Christmas, sister," she says, offering her cheek for a kiss. Her voice is stronger this morning. I am certain of it.

"Isn't this a Christmas miracle?" I embrace her. My ear to hers, I hear the sound of the ocean. I draw back with a start.

"Doesn't she look lovely?" Auntie says. She sets a steaming plate of scones on the table beside jewel-colored jam and a saucer of pale yellow butter. "I brewed up a tisane of dried kelp, crushed shark's tooth, and powdered mussel shells. Perked her right up."

"And look!" Maren points to the window. "It's snowing."

Osbert stretches his long neck to get a glimpse of the weather. His barbed tail bounces up and down, drumming a happy beat on the floorboards. Our wyvern loves to play in the snow.

"After breakfast, could Clara harness Osbert to the little sleigh and take me for a ride to the meadow?" Maren asks. "Please? I feel ever so much better, Auntie."

"Well, maybe for a few minutes. Girls of your particular temperament are not meant for the snow, Maren dear."

"I am not a mermaid yet, Auntie." Her familiar pout returns. It makes my heart sing to see her so much herself again.

"I suppose," Auntie says. "But just a short ride, mind you. We have Christmas gifts to open."

Maren and I wolf down our breakfasts. Auntie indulges our lack of manners. In her eyes I see her thought: *This will be Maren's last Christmas with us.* And Auntie cannot tell a lie, cannot even think one.

Auntie wraps Maren in coats and capes and every spare blanket she can find. Outside, I buckle the red leather harness around the exuberant wyvern. His wings flap snow into my eyes. His wagging tail has swept three inches of snow from the ground to reveal sprigs of brown grass.

Together, Auntie and I settle Maren into the sleigh. She is light as a feather, even covered in woolens and down-filled quilts. Her sparkling face peers out of Auntie's paisley shawl. Has anyone ever been more beautiful than my sister?

"Just a short trip," Auntie cautions as I lead Osbert across our white-clothed garden.

After the kitchen door shuts with a thud, there is silence—the holy silence of winter, broken only by the pings of snowflakes meeting their siblings on the ground, and the soft shushing of the sleigh.

The glorious meadow twinkles and glimmers in its winter finery. Towering pines stand at its edges like ermine-clad kings. Maren sighs and squeezes my mittened hand. We do not need to speak.

From a distance, a sound reaches my ears. First, it seems like the scratching of some animal's claws against metal. As it grows, I recognize the sound of bells.

"The Halsteds must be taking a sleigh ride," I remark. But a moment later, a small horse trots out of the forest, his black coat almost painful to behold against the white snow. His mane is woven with silver bells and ribbons, and on his back he wears fat saddlebags of green leather, but no saddle. He stops when he sees us and bows his head as if in greeting. Steam rises from his nostrils in roiling clouds.

"He is darling!" Maren says. Her voice is muffled by a thick, woolen scarf.

"You poor, frozen dear," I say to the horse. "Follow us and we will warm you by our fire." I shake the reins. "Home, Osbert." The horse trails behind the sleigh, his bells jingling merrily.

"What have we here?" Auntie says from the doorway. "The poor creature! Bring him in before he freezes solid!"

The horse just fits through the kitchen door. Auntie stations him by the fire as if he were a human friend come to call and not an animal that ought to be in the barn. Next we carry Maren in. She is squirming with delight, enthralled by our odd Christmas visitor.

Once Maren is comfortably arranged in the rocker, I shed my coat and scarf and set to rubbing the horse dry. He nickers and nods with gratitude.

"Now, my fine fellow," Auntie says, "might we see what you carry in your pack? Perhaps a clue as to where you ought to be this grand day."

The horse nickers again and shakes his mane of silver bells. After Auntie takes the pack from his back, she sets it on the kitchen table. I work to undo one of the buckles and Auntie works at the other. With sleepy eyes, Maren watches us from the fireside. The horse lies down and places his head next to her steaming footbath.

"You do the honors," Auntie says to me, stepping aside.

I open the flap. On top of several brown-papered boxes, I find an envelope. "Mrs. Verity Amsell and Nieces," it reads. I gasp, recognizing the loopy penmanship. No one but O'Neill has such a hand. "It's from O'Neill. But how?" I say excitedly.

"Open it and see, for goodness' sake," Auntie urges.

Inside, I find two letters. One is addressed to "Mrs. V. Amsell, and also the Young Misses Maren and Clara." The other is addressed solely to me. I slip my letter into my skirt pocket before tearing open the letter to us all. I read it aloud.

Dear ones,

I beg your forgiveness for our lack of correspondence, and most especially for not returning in October as is our habit. Scarff and I have been beset by ill luck since leaving you last summer. We have been burglarized, we suffered two broken wheels in the space of a week, and we capsized in a river—a harrowing adventure I will expound upon when I see you again. We also lost our way in a most peculiar forest for nine days, and recently, both came down with a terrible fever, which even Auntie Verity's best elixirs could not eradicate. As I write this, Job and January are fighting off some sort of equine cough.

We are currently camping with a band of jovial gypsies on the banks of an alligator-infested lake. They are good with the horses (the gypsies, not the alligators). Madame Vadoma burns the foulest of incense, swearing that it will keep the toothy reptiles at bay. Yet I do not trust the beasts (the alligators, not the gypsies). There is hunger in their eyes and ill will in their toothy grins.

Through all of this, our hearts have been constantly aching to return to you, our dearest friends. How we have fretted over Maren's health! To that effect, we have enclosed a few items she may find helpful. You will find them in the small square box.

Scarff begs me to inform you, Auntie, that when we return in spring, he will bring you the one thing your heart and his have most greatly desired for all your years of acquaintance. He says this with an impish smile and will tell me no more of it.

Since you are reading this, you have met our friend Zedekiah. I am confident that he will enjoy life with you on Llanfair Mountain, as he has a great affinity for clovers drenched in dew.

Scarff and I send our love to you all. If wishing got a body something, we would wish to spend this Christmas in your snug cottage. And now I am imagining Auntie's delectable pies and hot spiced cider and drooling on my best waistcoat. Scarff bids me to stop immediately.

Your faithful servants,
O'Neill the Magnificent and Ezra Scarff

"Gypsies and alligators," Maren whispers. "Can it be true?"

"Of course it is," I say. "Why would O'Neill make up such a tale?"

"To impress us with his brave exploits," she says.

Her words awaken a defensiveness of O'Neill I had not realized was lurking in my heart. I open my mouth to rebuke my sister, but Auntie interrupts.

"Shall we see what gifts they sent? Poor Zedekiah carried the burden of them for hundreds of miles, and yet it seems that you girls would rather bicker than open them." Auntie has her hands on her hips in her best "maternal authority" pose.

Without another word, I peel the brown paper from the first box and remove its lid. Inside are smaller boxes, each adorned with a gilt-edged tag naming the recipient.

I deliver Maren's into her hands. She smiles, the sparkles around her eyes glistening. We silently forgive one another for our squabbling.

Within my sister's little box is a necklace: a gold locket engraved with an apple tree. She sighs and presses it to her breast before slipping the delicate chain over her head.

Auntie coos over her gift: an illuminated book of herbal recipes collected in a volume small enough to fit in her apron pocket. "So pretty and practical at the same time," she declares.

Holding my breath, I open the box meant for me. I am ready to be amazed. And ready to be disappointed.

Wrapped in crinkly paper is a miniature painting in a wooden frame. It could easily fit inside a soup spoon. I hold the scene close and examine its subjects: a white stork perched in a fruit-laden tree, a rippled pond. At the edge of the pond, almost too small to see, is a pink conch shell.

Auntie leans in over my shoulder. "O'Neill painted that himself," she says. "He was working on it in August when he was here. My, how lovely! Such a talented boy!"

I cannot decide whether I am pleased with my gift or jealous of Maren's. I despise myself for such selfishness. Does not my sister deserve all of the best gifts? Her time with us seems to be dwindling so quickly. She may not spend another Christmas with Auntie and me. She may never celebrate the holidays again, for who knows what customs mermaids keep?

From each of Maren's ocean-colored eyes falls a pearl the size of the head of a pin. They roll down her pale, twinkling cheeks, over the smooth silk of her robe, and tumble to the floor. She does not try to catch them. "I will miss Christmas most, of all the days in the year," she says, as if she has read my mind.

"Come now," Auntie says. "We must not dwell on what will or will not be. Today we have Christmas. Today is all we have, my dears. Today is all we ever have." Despite her brave words, Auntie has tears in her eyes as well.

Outside, Osbert scratches at the door and howls. In all the excitement over Zedekiah, we left our faithful wyvern in the snow. Auntie lifts the latch and he bolts across the kitchen, dragging a snowdrift in with his tail. Little icicles hang from his chin like a beard. His wings stick out stiffly at his sides. Maren laughs as he turns three circles in front of the fire and flops onto his belly with a pitiful moan.

Auntie places a basin of warm peppermint tea under Osbert's snout. "Merry Christmas to you, beast," she says. "There's your favorite."

After we open the other packages (a tin of dried seaweed, six oranges, several yards of scarlet and black brocade, two drawing pencils, a harmonica, eight well-polished clamshells, and a jar of vanilla beans), I slip away to the bedroom to read my letter from O'Neill.

Perched on the edge of the bed, I stare at the loops and swirls that make up my name. What was he thinking when he penned the letters? That he missed me? That he missed his almost-sister? Or that he needed to hurry and get to his chores, or into the arms of some lovely gypsy girl?

My trembling fingers pry the flap loose and the letter falls into my lap. The folded paper is onion-skin thin. Words crisscross over words like the dark tracks of ice skates upon a frozen pond.

With great care, I coax the missive flat and begin to read.

Dear Clara,

I hope this letter finds you well, and that Zedekiah has arrived before Christmas. He promised to do his utmost to reach you before December's end.

I am writing to you privately because I do not wish to alarm Auntie. But I feel compelled to tell you the truth, dearest friend. That truth is, Scarff is quite unwell. The fever has left him weak as a kitten, yet he manages to cough as if he might bring up a lung. His clothes are suddenly too large for him. I wish that I could deliver him into Auntie's care, as I know she could fatten him up and restore his vim and vigor in no time. Unfortunately, Scarff is constrained by rules that you and I cannot comprehend, rules that dictate the days and seasons he may set foot upon your splendid mountain. This is a mystery to me, as I know it is to you. In Auntie's stead, the incense-burning gypsy Madame Vadoma looks after him in her way. She is a hundred years old if she is a day, and seems to have a way with medicines and charms. Scarff is as gruff as a bear with her, but it only makes her cackle.

How I miss you and Maren! My greatest fear is that the mermaid will overtake her before I return. I enclose Madame Vadoma's receipt for a tisane that she claims will slow the transformation, and ease any pain Maren might have. I beg you to try it (with Auntie's permission, of course).

Please tear the receipt from this letter and then burn it. (I mean burn the letter, not the receipt.)

In the spring, we will dance in the orchard with the honeybees. I will teach you how to eat fire and throw knives (skills my gypsy friends have taught me). These things I swear, dear Clara, by all the alligators in the lake.

Your faithful servant,
O'Neill

Madame Vadoma's Receipt for Maren

2 teaspoons dried seaweed
Shredded rind of ½ orange
1 teaspoon dried lavender flowers
½ teaspoon salt (preferably sea salt)
2 pinches of crushed clamshell (use mortar and pestle to make
*   like sand)*
1 strand of hair from the Person Who Needs This Medicine
Dash of black pepper

Tie ingredients inside a square of cotton cloth and steep in 1 cup of boiled water for 5 minutes. Add 1 teaspoon of honey and drink all within 3 minutes with eyes closed and a silver coin in left hand. Drink once before breakfast and once at bedtime.

I read the letter again and again. Why does O'Neill's odd penmanship make it difficult for me to breathe?

In spite of his instructions, I tear the letter into three pieces. One is the receipt to give to Auntie, one is the paragraph in which O'Neill promises to dance with me and teach me to eat fire, and one is the rest of the letter. I set the receipt on the nightstand. I tuck the paragraph about dancing and fire-eating beneath my pillow. I toss the largest section into the coals of the bedroom's fireplace and watch as the paper turns gray and then black before bursting into flame.

Watching the flames, I picture O'Neill. He extends his arms and I step into them as a shower of apple blossoms descends around us. He begins to hum, and we waltz around the apple tree. There is no one else in the world but us, and I am happy.

It is one more wish for my collection.

Auntie is asleep in her chair by the fire, her embroidery hoop in her lap. Osbert snores beside Maren's footbath. Maren hums softly, a song I do not know. If I had to give it words, it would tell of undersea princesses riding dolphins to their undersea weddings.

My sister seems content. Perhaps it is only my imagination, but I think her countenance has brightened since Auntie dosed her with Madame Vadoma's tisane—although less than an hour has passed since Maren drank the murky, dark-green liquid.

A glint of gold on the mantel shelf catches my eye. Gold ribbon wrapped around a tiny cherrywood box. Simon's Christmas gift to Maren! How could I have forgotten it all this time?

I take the box down and give it to Maren. A note is tucked beneath the ribbon.

"Will you read it, sister?" Maren asks. "Reading tires me so." I can see several rows of silver-edged scales through the fabric of her nightgown, ending just above the curve of her hip. She never wears a proper dress anymore; a corset would be unbearable, for it would crush her new scales. Besides, mermaids were not meant for clothes. Even the thinnest of nightgowns seems to irritate her.

I unfold the note. "Are you sure I should read it? It is from Simon. It may be private."

"Read," she says. She closes her eyes, and I begin.

Dearest darling Maren,

Here is a gift for you. It is very special. I bought it at the medicine show on the second night, when you were not with me, from the woman who sang and almost sold us gloves. She said it was from her country, and that if you kept it close to you, it would ease any sufferings you might have. She seemed to think you were unwell. Regardless, I thought it pretty. But not as pretty as you, my dearest darling.

Ever yours,
Simon David Shumsky

I groan. "Dearest darling? Ugh."

"He cannot help his feelings, I suppose," Maren says. She lifts the lid of the box and takes out a small stone. It is deep brown with a stripe of bronze down the center, like the eye of a cat. "It is rather pretty." She pries open the locket O'Neill sent and places the stone inside. "It will be safe there, and if it has the magic the woman said it does, it will be close enough to me to do its work. Perhaps it *will* lessen the pain of changing. At times it is almost more than I can bear."

"I will be glad if it helps you. But I do not think that anything they sold at the show was genuine," I say. "Remember how Auntie had to make special tonics for many of the villagers who took Dr. Phipps's mixtures?"

Maren yawns. "Yes. But this is only a bit of rock. What harm could it do?"

Auntie awakens with a start. "Goodness me, it's nigh on midnight. Time for bed, my girls."

Auntie and I each put an arm about Maren's shoulders and help her hobble to bed. We wrap her greenish-blue legs in damp towels and kiss her good night.

"Merry Christmas, sister," Maren and I say at the same moment. A tiny pearl rolls down Maren's cheek and onto her pillow.

I lie down with her and press my hand against her cool, glittering cheek. "We have had the best of Christmases, haven't we, dear? Snow and gifts from Scarff and O'Neill, that funny little horse, and Auntie's good food. I am grateful for it, and you." I swallow hard, tasting unshed tears in the back of my throat.

She closes her eyes. "I wonder if they celebrate Christmas beneath the sea. If *I* will." Her voice is fading again. Whatever Christmas miracle returned it to her is diminishing.

"That is a mystery," I say. "A very great mystery."

Next year, unless O'Neill procures a very great miracle to reverse the change, she will know for certain what the merfolk do at Christmas. Will she send a message by seagull to share with me the customs they keep in the deep? Will she send gifts of sea glass and pirates' lost coins? Will she remember us at all?

Time will tell.

CHAPTER EIGHT

In my nighttime dreams, I am brave.

Maren rides behind me on Zedekiah. He is not the small horse who has taken up residence in the barn with our three goats. He is a splendid stallion, sixteen hands high, regal and fearless. He carries us over mountains and through rivers, across barren plains and through tangled forests.

I sit up as straight and tall as a princess, but I am dressed as a boy, and a long sword bounces against my leg with each of Zedekiah's prancing steps. We journey through many days and nights until we reach the sea.

Zedekiah gallops into the water. He slows as the water reaches his chest, and stops altogether when it reaches the base of his neck.

Something is approaching, moving fluidly toward us, moving fast under a layer of water as thin as glass. I draw my sword.

Out of the water appears the head of a giant sea horse, and enthroned upon the sea horse is a bare-chested man. Or rather, a bare-chested merman. His hair is white and as wild as the waves, and his crown is made of coral and pearls. His fishy half starts just below his navel, scales of iridescent green and orange and gold.

His brow is furrowed, but he is smiling. "Daughter?" he says, his ocean-colored eyes on my sister. He urges the sea horse closer and reaches for Maren.

"Stand down," I command. "We have not come to surrender, but to demand that you release her from your realm. We demand that you grant her freedom from the sea and return her to her human form." My sword is pointed at his head. I do not tremble before this king.

He laughs with the sound of a thousand waves crashing into the sands of a thousand beaches. Still, I neither tremble nor back down. "Release her," I say. "Or your blood shall mingle with these waters."

With a slap of his tail, the merman bids the sea horse to charge. He raises his trident and in that instant, I swipe at him with my sword.

I miss.

The points of his trident press into my chest. "Silly girl," he bellows. "Would you exchange your life for her freedom?"

"Yes," I say without hesitation. "Yes."

"So be it," he says. He draws his weapon back and then thrusts it toward my heart.

I awaken with a start and a cry.

Could I ever be as brave as the dream version of myself? I do not believe so.

The kitchen is quiet, save for the crackle of the fire, the arrhythmic clicking of my knitting needles, and the occasional swish of pages being turned by Auntie. Maren dozes in the rocker, and Osbert huddles beside her soaking feet.

Perhaps the foot-deep layer of snow on and about our cottage conceals the sound of Simon Shumsky's carriage. Perhaps Osbert has fallen into some sort of wyvern hibernation. Regardless, Osbert does not provide his usual warning of unwanted company.

The knock on the door sends him flying to the cellar.

"Oh, my stars," Auntie says as she gets to her feet. "He's here. To take our Maren to the dance!"

"We must get rid of him before he sees her!" I say.

The door is thrown open. "Good evening, ladies," Simon says, stepping into the kitchen. He wears a new coat and hat, and an eager smile. "Is Maren ready?"

Somehow (miracle of miracles!), he does not notice Maren fast asleep under her mound of dampened shawls.

To distract him, I say, "Let me make you a cup of tea. You must be half-frozen." I take his arm and direct him to a seat at the table.

"Dear heavens," Auntie says. "I hate to disappoint you, Simon, especially since you came all this way in the cold."

"But she is better now, isn't she?" His brow furrows with what I read as worry mixed with frustration.

"No, Simon. She is still unwell. I have done all that I can, but she is not fit to go out in the cold. She is in no way strong enough for dancing," Auntie says gently but firmly.

I set the tea in front of him. "We should have sent word. We are very sorry. There will be other dances," I say. Other dances for him, but not for Maren.

Auntie pulls a chair close to him. "Simon, may I speak plainly?"

He nods and drinks down his tea as though it is medicine.

"Maren has a condition of which she cannot be cured. I know that you love her, but I must tell you that she can never marry any man," Auntie says in her most soothing voice.

Fat tears stand at the edges of Simon's eyes. "Never?"

"What is worse, Simon, is that I must ask you not to visit again. She will become rather disfigured, and I know it would distress her to have you see her in such a state."

One great sob escapes Simon before he regains his composure. "Forgive me," he says.

"There is nothing to forgive," I say. "Why should you ask forgiveness for being devoted to Maren? For loving her?"

"I am sorry," he says. He stands and walks toward the door like a sleepwalker. He does not say good-bye and forgets to close the door behind him.

Osbert creeps up from the cellar. Auntie shuts the door and sighs. "The poor man. His heart is broken."

"Was that true love, Auntie?" I pick up Simon's empty cup.

"Indeed," she says.

I wish . . .

I do not know what I wish.

Chapter Nine

A peculiar change in the weather melts all the snow on New Year's Day and brings another pair of visitors to our cottage.

With a basket containing three eggs (and we are lucky the winter-hating chickens produced that many), I walk the gravel path between the henhouse and the cottage. Presently, I hear the wheels of an approaching wagon, but, alas, the music of odd chimes and banging pots does not accompany it. It is the wagon belonging to Peterman and Sons, the village's general store.

Mr. Peterman, a spry gentleman on the far side of sixty, jumps down from the seat as nimbly as a cat. His plump son Henry Donald heaves himself to the frozen ground with a thud.

"Good afternoon, gentlemen," I say. "What brings you up the mountain?"

"Oh, it is good to see you, Miss Clara," Mr. Peterman says, grinning, doffing his hat. "Nothing like a pretty girl to warm a man's chilled heart and soul."

"Hullo, Miss Clara," Henry Donald says. His chapped cheeks redden further as he stares at his boots, the image of a schoolboy caught with a love letter. The poor fellow is forty years old and as shy as a fawn.

"There you are!" Auntie calls from the doorway. "Have you brought my special order?"

"Yes, ma'am," Mr. Peterman replies. "It arrived at the store a week ago, but with the weather being such as it was, we couldn't get up here till now."

Auntie and I watch as the two men place planks from the wagon bed to the ground to form a ramp. At Henry Donald's count of three, they lift a large wooden crate and carry it off the wagon.

"Where do you want it, Mrs. Amsell?" Mr. Peterman asks as he walks backward toward the cottage.

"Well, for now you can put it in the girls' room," Auntie says. She opens the door wide and steps aside. "Straight through there," she says. "The room on the left just after the grandfather clock."

With groans and scrapings of doorways, the Petermans reach their destination. I follow them, wondering what the box might hold—and where my sister is hiding.

Mr. Peterman takes a hammer from his belt and uses its claw end to pry off the top of the crate, and then to pry apart the sides. The wood falls away to reveal a six-foot-long metal tub, dark silver inside and painted pine-green on the outside.

"That's a beauty," Mr. Peterman says, patting the edge. "If my wife were to catch sight of it, she'd take a notion to get one for herself."

"It is quite pretty," Auntie says. "And it should do our Maren a world of good. She has troubles with her legs and feet, you see, and nothing makes her feel better than a good soak. Now come into the kitchen and have a nice hot cup of tea and some raisin cake before you go."

After Auntie ushers Mr. Peterman and Henry Donald into the kitchen, I climb into the tub. Imagine! A bathtub! We have never had such a luxury, but have never wanted it, either. Our warm weather bathing has always consisted of joyful splashing in the creek, and in wintertime we squeeze ourselves into the wash-tub once a week. I imagine steaming water swirling about me, the scent of Auntie's good lavender soap . . . and then I remember what Auntie said about Maren and her "troubles." And I realize that this tub is not for baths. It will be Maren's home, like a fishbowl for a half-fish girl.

Leaving the tub behind, and not liking it half so much as I had at first, I tiptoe across the hall to Auntie's tiny bedroom. "There you are," I say to Maren. She is lying on Auntie's bed, wrapped in wet towels. Her eyes are half-closed. From the end of the towels protrudes a single silver-green fin. My stomach lurches. Without asking permission, I peel back the towels to look at what should be two feet and two legs.

"Oh, Maren," I sigh. "My poor sister." Tears fall from my eyes and splatter upon her fused-together legs, a single limb embel-lished with rows of small, glassy scales, like the ones that first appeared on her sides last summer.

"Don't cry, Clara," she whispers. Her voice is the swish of sea foam on sand.

"Your poor legs." I stroke what used to be her pale calf.

"They hurt less now that they are one."

I shake my head. I have no words. Carefully, I climb onto the bed and nestle beside her, my head on her damp shoulder. And silently I weep for her loss. For my loss of her.

"Hush, now," she whispers in her gentle tide voice. "I must be what I am, dear, as much as it pains me to leave you."

"If only I was already a stork, if only I had wings to carry me, I would fly until I found a cure for you. I would fly until my last feather dropped to the earth."

"I know, sister. Hush, now. Can't you hear the sea birds' wings above us? Can you not hear the sailors singing as they unfurl their great sails? Can you not hear the low bellows of the whales speaking to their children in the deepest deep?"

No, I think. *I hear nothing but the sound of my heart breaking into a million tiny pieces, each smaller than a single grain of sand.*

Winter is long. Long, cold, dark, and tiresome. Not like our former winters, when we played checkers and knucklebones, made up two-person plays for Auntie's amusement, sang songs beside the fire, and attempted to learn French and lacemaking (both the lacemaking and the French studies proved abysmal failures). Not like the evenings when we planned aloud our futures, futures that more often than not involved marrying handsome foreigners and living in fine houses built side by side, our tribes of happy children frolicking in our shared gardens. Not like the evenings when Auntie would tell us fairy stories and stories of her youth—which sometimes seemed to overlap and entwine. Those were cozy, lovely, snug times in our cottage home.

These winter months, Maren reclines in the bathtub, day and night. She spends hours smoothing her lovely hair with the tortoiseshell comb O'Neill gave her for her sixteenth birthday. Day by day, her hair changes, growing longer and more coppery, speckled with glittery flecks. It cascades in waves over her shoulders and floats on the surface of the water like tendrils of an exotic vine. Auntie wraps Maren from underarms to waist in lengths of bright cotton "for modesty's sake," for the mermaid girl is now fully fish from the waist down and has no use for dresses or skirts.

"Is there nothing more you can do?" I ask Auntie for the thousandth time as we carry empty buckets back to the kitchen. "Is there no possible way to make her human again?" The foolish questions spill from my mouth although I know full well what Auntie will say: Maren never was, and never will be, truly human.

Nevertheless, I ask—because my heart and mind refuse to quit quarreling. Because love and truth are in a tangle that I wish to unravel.

"No, my girl." Auntie shakes her head sadly. "And I fear that she will soon sicken. Mermaids belong in the ocean, not the bath. If only Scarff were here to help us. Surely he could find a way to take her to her kind. But, alas, it is February, and he never comes before mid-March."

I bite my lower lip. If she had but an inkling of Scarff's condition, she might truly despair. "We must try to keep her well until he comes, then."

"Yes. I only hope that we are not causing her undue pain by giving her tisanes and potions to slow the change. Sometimes it is unwise to tamper with the inevitable."

"I do not think she has much pain anymore. Whenever I catch her crying, she says it is only because she is homesick for the sea."

We set the buckets down and sit at the kitchen table.

"If I could leave this place . . ." Auntie says, her eyes awash with regret. "But I cannot."

"Perhaps I should try to take her," I say, well aware that Auntie has not set foot off the mountain since long before my birth. Indeed, the thought makes *my* stomach clench with fear, but I speak on. "The worst of winter is likely past, and the roads are clear enough for the wagon. Zedekiah is small, but he could manage to pull Maren and me. I could dress like a boy to be safe. And when O'Neill arrives, you could send him to join us." My voice sounds foreign to me, my words like someone else's.

Auntie wraps her wrinkled fingers about my wrist. "You do not have to prove your love for Maren to me, my dear. Nor to her. Let us wait a little longer for Scarff and O'Neill. If they do not appear by March, I will consider your offer." She smiles faintly, whether to reassure herself or me, I cannot tell.

I attempt a smile of my own—for Auntie's sake alone. "I know you have done everything you could for Maren, Auntie. I only want to be able to say the same for myself."

She neither agrees nor disagrees, just pats my shoulder. "I will make tea," she says. "And we will cling to what hope we have."

The days are a blur of repetition. I read to Maren. I sing to her. She smiles wistfully when I recount our childhood adventures, especially ones involving the mischief O'Neill always got us into. While she naps, I clasp her damp hand and daydream of happier times.

I admit that I daydream of O'Neill more than any other subject. Perhaps more than I should. But thoughts of him shore up my heart with moments of much-needed joy. I think perhaps I love him more each day. Is that how true love works? I will not ask Auntie.

Every few hours, I scoop buckets of cooled water from the tub and refill it with water from the kettles Auntie heats continually on the woodstove. I add handfuls of coarse salt. When people come up from the village in need of remedies, Auntie closes the bedroom door firmly, with a discreet turning of key in lock, saying that Maren is "not her *usual* self." Auntie always tells the truth.

One afternoon, while Auntie is filling bottles of cough elixir in the kitchen, Maren naps, and I am drowsing over *Robinson Crusoe*, a tapping at our bedroom window startles me. Just the wind, I think. I begin to reread page thirty-seven for what must be the thirty-seventh time. And then it happens again. Turning my head, I see a dark shape outside the frost-starred pane.

After setting the book on the mattress, I tiptoe to the window. The tapping is *pecking*, I realize as I discern the outline of a bird. As soon as I open the window, the bird swoops into the room, accompanied by a bone-chilling blast of wind. With all my strength, I push the pane back into place and turn the latch.

Awakened by the commotion, Maren watches the raven perch on the edge of the tub and bow its head in salute. She applauds and laughs in tiny gasps. I have not seen her so delighted since her last autumn's swim in the Wishing Pool.

"Kraa," calls the raven, shaking one leg in my direction. Tied to the leg with a red string is a piece of brown paper.

"What have you here?" I say to the bird as I work to undo the complicated knot. "Sorry, Mr. Raven. I'm doing my best." Finally, the string gives way and the paper slips to the floor.

"A message?" Maren asks in her soft, ocean-breeze voice.

"We shall see." I retrieve the paper and it unfolds itself in the palm of my hand like an enchanted flower. I recognize the handwriting immediately and my heart rejoices. "It is from O'Neill!"

Maren claps her hands, sending water drops flying onto the raven and me. "Read it," she mouths. "Out loud."

"Of course," I reply. "The message says . . . oh, my! Such small print!" I bring the paper closer to my face and angle it to catch the firelight. "There," I say, and begin.

Dear Clara, Maren, and Verity,

I present to you the good raven Pilsner. He is a gift from our gypsy friends, a bird of extraordinary talent. He brings to you our fondest greetings and our news. And our news is this: Scarff is much improved, and Job and January in fine fettle. We leave here very soon, and hope to be with you by first of March. We beseech you, dear ladies, to keep well until we meet again. And ever after, of course.

Yours faithfully,
O'Neill, and Scarff also

Carrie Anne Noble

Postscript: Pilsner has a great fondness for cheese, the sharper the better.

With a contented smile and a wriggle of her mermaid tail, Maren sinks a bit lower into the water. Pilsner hops along the edge of the tub until he reaches the point closest to the fireplace. He ruffles his feathers and closes his eyes, his task well done.

O'Neill is coming, my heart sings. In two short weeks, he will be here with us. In spite of Auntie's predictions of Maren's fate, I dare to hope that he might rescue us from our loss of her yet, that he might bring a charm or a potion or *something* that will make her fully human again. That he will be the hero who can change this tale of woe into a happily-ever-after story.

Perhaps I am a fool.

No, I *know* I am a fool. Why else would I keep wishing for a way for Maren to become a girl again when Auntie's wise words echo in my head a hundred times each day: "There is no cure for being who you truly are."

Why else would I wish something for my sister that she does not wish for herself?

Maren flicks her tail and droplets of water fly into my face. Her eyes twinkle with mischief. "You look far too glum for having read such good news," she whispers. She flings another fin-full of water my direction and drenches my dress.

I grab the pitcher from the washstand and empty it over Maren's head.

She pushes wet strands of hair away from her eyes and laughs, a sound like little waves lapping at pebbles. "That was nice," she says. "Lovely."

She extends a hand and I take it. For a moment we are nothing but the sisters we have been for seventeen years.

Without warning, she yanks hard, pulling me into the tub with her. We laugh ourselves breathless, and then lie still. She holds me in her arms and I do not struggle. The water is warm and my sister's embrace is a rare and sweet thing.

"I wish you were a mermaid," Maren whispers.

I close my eyes and try to think of how to answer her, but words fail me.

CHAPTER TEN

Pilsner follows Auntie about like a winged, two-legged puppy. He is utterly devoted to her, as she was to him after a mere hour of acquaintance. She feeds him bits of our best cheese, morsels of apples and pears, and wee griddle cakes studded with sunflower seeds and raisins—all arranged prettily on a blue-flowered saucer. At night, he perches on her bedpost like a black-plumed guardian angel.

And as O'Neill said in his note, Pilsner is a bird of extraordinary talent. If his only talents had been the finding of dropped sewing needles and lost buttons (besides the delivery of letters from afar), he would have been amazing enough. But he is also a fine opponent at checkers, and a gifted dancer. His best talent of all, however, is making our Maren laugh.

Osbert's jealousy is both pitiful and comical. His attempts to be a lap dog are ridiculous. Who wants to cuddle a hundred-pound dragon, for goodness' sake? His mournful whimpering for attention is most unwyvernlike. Occasionally, I catch him eyeing the bird with a hungry look and remind him that he is the one who chose to be a domestic creature, and therefore must not give way to his wild urges.

Amusing ravens and envious wyverns aside, I am worried.

Worried because it is now the second week of March and Scarff and O'Neill have not yet rattled and clanged their way to our gate. But more worried because I am certain that my sister is *shrinking*.

Auntie sees it, too, I know. Although she has not said a word about it, I have watched Auntie run her gaze along the length of our mermaid girl, shaking her head and clucking her tongue.

Auntie lifts one of Maren's hands and kisses her pale, glittery skin. Maren stirs but keeps her mother-of-pearl colored eyelids closed. Auntie's brow furrows with concern and sorrow. She sprinkles a teacupful of salt into the tub and stirs it with her hand, swirling the warm water and causing Maren's floating locks to tangle.

My sister is no longer human. From her coppery hair to the end of her glorious, iridescent tail, Maren is a mermaid. She is beautiful in a way that no mere human could ever be. The only remnants of humanness she retains are O'Neill's locket (which she refuses to remove), and the shawl that covers her breasts.

I will not ask, "How long can she survive this way?" or "Is she truly growing smaller each day?" I fear Auntie's utterly honest answers. And in my heart of hearts, I *know* what they would be.

Osbert nuzzles my leg with his snout and I scratch him between his pointy ears. He could live five hundred more years, he could grow bigger than the cottage and boast teeth as tall as O'Neill, but he will never forget any of this. Wyverns never forget a thing, not even silly pet wyverns like our Osbert.

Suddenly, he lifts his head and perks his ears. His wings twitch and his tail slaps the hardwood floor. With a hearty howl, he dashes into the kitchen and berates the door for being shut. In between his complaints and barks, I hear the faint sound of pots and pans banging together, the tinkle of many wind chimes. My heart races so that I can barely catch my breath.

Auntie is on her feet before I can persuade my own feet to move. Happy tears stream over her plump cheeks as she gives me a gentle shove. "Go on, girl," she says. "Hurry out and welcome the wanderers home. Thank heavens the winter is finally over!"

Osbert and I race to the wagon, with Pilsner soaring above us. As soon as O'Neill's boots meet the ground, I throw myself into his arms.

"Well," he says, "I did not expect such a welcome from you, my well-mannered lass."

"Thank you, thank you," I say into his shoulder, breathing in that O'Neill scent I have missed: spices and strong soap, sun-dried clothes and happiness. I feel rescued and hopeful—and in love. "I thought you'd never come."

He pats my back. "Ah, but I always do, don't I? As surely as the spring, Scarff and I always return to our girls."

I step out of his embrace, still clutching the fabric of his colorful vest, and I look into his face. "It was silly of me to think otherwise." I blush like Mr. Peterman's awkward son and let go of his clothes.

"You're even prettier than the last time I saw you, Miss Clara," he teases.

"And you've grown taller, haven't you? Has Scarff been forced to buy you new trousers again?"

O'Neill holds out a leg. "He gave me his old boots instead. Says people won't notice how short my trousers are if my boots go to my knees."

Scarff and Auntie face one another, holding hands. She is fussing over his gauntness, the hollows in his cheeks, the thinness of his pale wrists, how his beard needs trimming and his jacket needs mending. He smiles like a leprechaun beholding an overflowing pot of gold.

"Take me to Maren," O'Neill says, tugging me along by the hand.

"You will not like what you see," I warn as we cross the threshold into the kitchen. "She is quite changed, O'Neill."

"Madame Vadoma's receipt did not work?"

"It helped a little. Have you brought nothing else for her? A charm or another receipt?"

He shakes his head. "The gypsies had nothing else to offer. I'm sorry."

From the doorway of the bedroom, the back of Maren's gold-speckled hair is just visible above the edge of the tub. He releases my hand and approaches her slowly, each step noiseless. When he rounds the tub and sees her fully, all color drains from his face.

"O'Neill," she mouths, her voice all but gone. Joy expands across her features, making her skin sparkle even more than usual.

"Oh, love," he whispers. He falls to his knees and reaches for her, cupping her cheek in his palm. "Look at you."

Maren lifts her silvery-green fin from the water, without any indication of regretting its presence. In fact, she seems proud of her strange appendage. "Beautiful," she mouths.

O'Neill stares at her in wide-eyed wonder. "Does it hurt? Are you in pain, dearest?"

She shakes her pretty head and motions with her hands. She touches her heart, then points outward, then pantomimes the waves of the ocean.

"She longs for the ocean," I translate. "She's been losing her voice." But I do not think he hears me. Every bit of his attention is directed toward Maren, and I cannot mistake the presence of pure love in his gaze and his gestures.

How I hate myself in this moment. I hate that I am jealous of his undisguised devotion. I hate that I love him and that he does not return my love. I hate that I can so easily think of myself and my desires when my sister is in danger of dying. I leave the room. What is between them is not meant for spectators.

I wish . . .

I wish, above all things, that none of this had ever happened.

Grateful that Scarff and O'Neill have brought sunshine with them, we throw open all the doors and windows to let in the warm air and the sounds of birds rejoicing. Auntie bustles about, gathering ingredients and supplies to prepare a celebratory feast. At Auntie's command, I stir and knead, baste and slice, chop and arrange. She alternately hums and fusses over the food. Will there be enough applesauce? Are those carrots cut thinly enough? Does O'Neill still hate cabbage?

Scarff and O'Neill are entertaining Maren. For once, she is wide awake and able to enjoy herself. Scarff's terrible jokes follow close upon O'Neill's fervent ballad singing (slightly off-key but still moving). Scarff's deep voice echoes through the cottage as he tells outrageous tales of his youth—which may or may not be true.

When the air is saturated with the scents of ham and fresh bread rolls, candied carrots and apple pie, and once the perfect sprig of parsley is plucked from its pot on the windowsill and placed atop the steaming platter of potatoes, Scarff and O'Neill drag Maren's tub into the kitchen—mermaid and all. She is given a view of the table and a cup of seaweed tea, for she no longer eats anything.

Other than the bathtub in the kitchen, the celebration resembles every other return-of-Scarff-and-O'Neill party we have ever had—complete with overeating and the exchange of stories and fond glances. Finally, Scarff stands and raises his glass of elderberry wine.

"A toast to the present company," he declares. We clink glasses and take sips, despite our full bellies. "Now, an announcement."

Maren claps her hands. Water droplets splash into the fireplace, hissing as they evaporate.

"For many long years has this wonderful creature been the very heart of my heart," he begins. He looks at Auntie as if they were both seventeen and stricken with first love.

"Do sit down," Auntie says, "and try not to embellish things too much!"

With a harrumph, Scarff settles into his chair beside Auntie. He takes her hand in his and rests them upon the table. "Shall I start at the very beginning, my love?"

Auntie nods, eyes twinkling.

Scarff leans back in his chair. "If I were to tell you how long ago this tale begins, you would doubt the entire telling of it. So, I will use the traditional beginning. Once upon a time, there was a beautiful young maiden."

Auntie rolls her eyes heavenward.

"'Tis true, 'tis true," Scarff insists. "No ordinary girl was she. It was said that her mother was of full faerie blood, and her father was a warrior prince of a far northern land. But she was placed in the care of a pair of spinster ladies. They raised her in a rambling redbrick mansion beside a blue lake. They taught her manners and dancing and how to sew a fine seam. What they did not teach her, what she already knew in her half-faerie bones, were the names and uses of every herb and plant in the forest. Why, without any lessons or books, the lass could make up medicines to cure almost anything. And when the spinster ladies—the Furstwangler sisters, they were called, Inga and Hilma—when they realized the depths of their adopted daughter's unusual talents, they sent her to be apprenticed to a healer woman in Bremen by the name of Frau Albruna. Some said Albruna was a witch, but I'd never call her such. She did not like the word, and crossing her never did anyone a lick of good. Well, our girl—who came to Albruna with the unlikely name of Veritude—had a mind like a thirsty sponge and before long she'd soaked up all Albruna had to teach. After that, young Fräulein Verity taught Albruna a thing or two!" Scarff pauses to sip his wine and wink at Auntie.

"Enough flirting," O'Neill scolds. "Get on with the story, old man."

"Yes. Well. Where was I? Oh, yes, Bremen. I was a strapping lad then, you see. Sixteen, and just back from a year at sea. I'd seen such things on that ship! Six-headed sea monsters that would give your Osbert nightmares! Squid bigger than the ship itself. And even mermaids, though none as lovely as our Maren."

Maren blows him a kiss. He pretends to catch and pocket it.

Scarff clears his throat and continues. "I was feeling poorly, so my grandmother sent me to Albruna's place on Otto Strasse. Now as world-traveled as I was, my first sight of Albruna gave me a fright. The tallest woman I'd ever laid eyes on, broad shouldered as the most strapping seaman, wild haired as Medusa, with eyes like two spheres of polished coal afire. I trembled in my boots. My mouth went dry and my pulse roared in my ears. Ready to die standing up, I was. And then a sweet voice came from behind the dreadful woman, saying, 'Who is it?' Like music, those three words. A second later, a face peered around the dreadful Albruna, and my poor heart stopped. Just stopped."

Auntie grins. "It stopped, and he fell like a sapling before a woodsman's ax. Flat onto Albruna's enormous feet, squashing her new doeskin slippers."

Scarff's chuckle rumbles like far-off thunder. "When I awoke, there was that beautiful face, peering into mine. My heart beating right as rain, but it no longer belonged to me, and never would again."

Auntie chimes in, "And I felt the same, from the moment I saw the scrawny blond boy all aquiver on Albruna's doorstep. Albruna knew it, too. She never said a word about it, but after we'd dosed our patient with tonics and tisanes for three days and nights, and the color had returned to his cheeks, she handed me a satchel holding all my earthly goods, placed a gold ring in Scarff's hand, and shooed us out the door as if we were a pair of trespassing chickens. I looked back from the street to see her wipe away a tear, and we waved good-bye to one another. I never saw her again."

Scarff lifts Auntie's hand to his lips and kisses her knuckles tenderly. "Before we took to the roads, we visited the old priest. Poor Father Matthias, as ancient and holy as he was, he greatly feared Albruna and her pupil, and so did not refuse to marry us—even though it was midnight, with only a pigeon in the chapel rafters as witness. Afterward, he gave us woolen blankets and a lantern and the room above his stables for the night."

"Married?" I exclaim in wonder and delight. "All this time!"

"You rascal," O'Neill says, poking Scarff in the shoulder. "Keeping such secrets from your own son!"

"Wait," I say. "Why have you not lived together? Why have we not all lived together? What fun we could have had!"

"If I could continue without you children interrupting, perhaps you might learn the answers to your questions." His tone is serious but his blue eyes merry.

"Do go on, forgiving us our rudeness," O'Neill says with false penitence.

"We wandered for years, my bride and I. I did odd jobs in the towns we visited, and Verity (no longer *Veritude*, since I changed her name on our wedding night), Verity earned coins aplenty healing the sick. A happier couple there never was. We had each other, a fine tent, a cooking pot, and all the world before us."

"Until?" offers O'Neill.

Caressing his fluffy beard thoughtfully, Scarff continues. "*Until*, my boy, until Verity and I took a notion to see the New World. The ships bobbing in the ocean in an English port sparked in her a longing to sail the seas. Remembering my seafaring youth more fondly than I should have, I agreed. Besides, I could deny the enchantress nothing. She might have slipped me a potion and made me into a hairy toad."

Scarff's wife (what a grand thing for Auntie to be Scarff's own *wife*!) slaps his arm playfully. "If only I could, you old buffoon!"

"Silliness aside," he says, "the crossing proved a nightmare. Half the passengers perished from a fever, and a third of the crew, as well. Verity nursed as many as she could, using up the box of herbs she'd brought, and much of the captain's own supply. Yet each morning brought the sounding of the ship's bell and splash after splash of shrouded bodies slipping into the sea. And days from America, the sickness ceased. For all but my wife, that is." He stops speaking and squeezes Auntie's hand.

O'Neill, ever the tease, says nothing. Maren rests her head against the back of the tub. Even Osbert and Pilsner seem to hold their breath in anticipation of Scarff's next words.

Finally, quietly, he continues. "My Verity fought the fever tooth and nail, and lived. But the child she bore did not. So tiny, she was, our daughter. Verity named her Violet and wrapped her in a length of snow-white silk. The sailors wept as the waves carried her little body away. We were all so heartsick that not one person cheered when we dropped anchor in Boston the following morning."

"Your only child," I whisper.

"Our *first* child, my dear," Auntie says. "The seashell, stork, and the apple tree gave us three more."

Standing and stretching like a bear fresh from hibernation, Scarff says, "It's late. I believe the rest of the story can wait until tomorrow."

O'Neill and I groan in unison. O'Neill says, "You didn't explain why you've lived apart. You can't leave us wondering!"

"I can and I will," Scarff says with authority. "Now, O'Neill my boy, hurry and fetch your things from the caravan. Tonight my darling wife will occupy your place in the bed. You may sleep in the kitchen or the barn, your choice."

Like a new bride, Auntie blushes. So do I.

"For heaven's sake," O'Neill grumbles. But he is smiling widely, looking just as happy as the old married couple. Or almost.

After the couple departs, O'Neill helps me replenish the warm water in Maren's tub. Next, I wash Maren's face and hands. It is silly, I know. She *lives* in clean water from the mountain springs and does nothing to become dirty. But we have always washed our faces together at bedtime. If we cannot share our bed anymore, cannot whisper secrets from our pillows or hold hands after nightmares, at least I can preserve a small piece of our former routine.

She is fast asleep before I finish dabbing the water from her alabaster cheeks; it would be pointless to move the tub back into the bedroom now. Osbert promises, with a nod of his head, to alert me if she needs anything during the night.

"That's done, then," O'Neill says as he places the last refilled kettle onto the stove. "I'll soon be off to the barn to share the hay with Zedekiah." He turns toward me, his expression strange and wistful. For a moment I think he might sweep me into his arms and kiss me, but no. His gaze is on the sleeping mermaid. His tender, loving gaze.

I drop my towel onto the table and hasten toward the bedroom. "Good night," I say without looking back.

"You don't want to stay up and talk? Like we always do? Come on, Clara. It is not even midnight."

"I am tired," I say. I close the door behind me and dive onto the bed, burying my anguish in the depths of my feather pillow.

I hate myself. I hate O'Neill.

I hate everything in the world. But mostly myself.

I dream.

My wings are long and white, with tips of black as if the feathers had brushed along a sea of ink. On ocean winds, I soar and circle. I angle my elegant red bill downwards and dive toward the water. A coppery head breaks through the top of a wave, and then the pale-skinned torso of a young woman: Maren. She reaches above her head with both arms and flips over into the churning ocean, her iridescent fish tail catching the sunlight before she disappears beneath the surf. My bill opens, but I cannot speak. No matter how I try, I can only make an ugly clattering sound. I dive after Maren, and the water swallows me up like a huge, toothless beast consuming its prey.

I awaken, my heart heavy. Is this prophecy, this strange dream? Will I truly be a stork, as Maren is a mermaid? Could it be confirmation of what I have long expected but attempted to ignore?

The truth is (in spite of all my attempts to ignore it), Maren has shown mermaid-like peculiarities since infancy: a love of water and a taste for salt, the uncanny ability to swim as deftly as a dolphin before she could even speak. But I am nothing like a stork. I haven't the slightest affinity for eating frogs and minnows, and have never desired to fly. My legs are not long, and I am far from graceful.

There, I tell myself. *I have examined the evidence and found good reason to declare that I will not become a stork.*

Then again, as Auntie has said, what I choose to believe does not change what is true.

I sigh with exasperation and roll onto what used to be Maren's side of the bed.

Through the window, the moon shines serenely. Its position in the sky tells me that dawn is many hours away. And so I count the stars, one by one, until somehow, I drift off to sleep again.

CHAPTER ELEVEN

A red sunrise stains the bedroom's lace curtains pink. I dress quickly, anxious to check on Maren. She is my first thought each day, even before I open my eyes. I do not think that I will ever grow accustomed to her sleeping in another room. Or another realm, for that matter.

So I go to her. And there, curled up beside the bathtub in a plaid blanket, is O'Neill. His hair sticks up like a field of wind-blown hay and he is snoring almost as loudly as Osbert, but to me he is beautiful.

I pinch my arm hard, punishing myself for my continued foolishness, for feeling so unsisterly toward my almost-brother. For being stupid enough to think he could ever choose me over Maren. My brown hair and eyes and regular features are perfectly unremarkable. She was always the pretty and charming one, and now in her mermaid state, she is glorious beyond words. What man could resist? Indeed, aren't mermaids supposed to be irresistible, capable of luring sailors to their deaths?

On my way to the stove, I bump into a chair. Its legs squeal as they scrape against the floor.

"Good morning," O'Neill says, his voice thick with sleep. "You are up with the chickens."

"Too cold in the barn?" Bitterness coats my words.

"Zedekiah was hogging the blankets. Are you angry with me? Was it terribly improper for me to sleep in the house?"

"Of course it was," I blurt. "And lying beside my sister! Just because she is a mermaid does not mean she should be treated like a harlot." I keep my face toward the window.

"I'm truly sorry," he says. "I did not think of that."

I let my emotions simmer for a moment. And then I take a deep breath. "I'm sorry, too," I say gently. "I should not have spoken to you like that."

"Friends?" he says. He is standing behind me now. The spicy Christmas scent of him still makes me woozy, no matter how I fight it.

"Of course," I say, pasting a smile on my face and turning around. "You are my almost-brother, after all."

Water whooshes and splashes against the inside of the tub as Maren stirs, attracting all our attention to the mermaid-girl.

O'Neill runs a hand through his hair, his habit when perplexed or troubled. He motions for me to follow him across the room, where Maren may not hear our whispers. "She is smaller than she was yesterday. I'm sure of it," he says.

I nod. "Every day, by fractions."

"What will become of her?"

"I think she must be taken to the ocean, or she will shrink away to nothing. She will disappear."

"We must take her, then." His eyes meet mine. "You and I must take her to the ocean. Scarff is not well enough, no matter what he might say. He needs to stay here with Auntie and her potions and recover his strength."

I know then, without a doubt, that he is as brave as the heroic O'Neill of my daydreams, braver than I could ever hope to be myself. "I will go with you," I say. *I would follow you to the ends of the earth*, I think. And then I look at the mermaid across the room. "I would do anything to save my sister."

"As would I," he says. He takes both my hands and squeezes them tightly. "We will make the journey together, and once there we will find a way to save her, Clara. Surely the merfolk can tell us how to release her from whatever enchantment has stolen her humanity."

The mermaid slaps her tail against the water. She points and gestures demandingly.

"Have patience, sister dear. I was just getting to that," I reply. "Fetch the buckets, O'Neill. Her highness requires fresh, warm water."

He bows low, with a flourish of his hand. "Queen Maren, your subjects shall obey."

She peers into O'Neill's face worshipfully as he scoops the old water from the tub to make room for the new. He meets her gaze and endows her with one of his mischievous, crooked grins before dousing her with the bucket's contents. She giggles (sea foam rolling over sand) and grabs his wrist and pulls. Only narrowly does he escape tumbling into the tub.

Maren's full-on laughter is a bubbling, subaquatic spring. Everything about her glistens: her skin, her copper-gold hair, the lustrous scales of her perfect tail. Even her eyes gleam. *She is happy.*

My sister, Maren, is happy as a mermaid. And she is happier still with O'Neill at her side. She has not shed a single pearl tear since his return to the mountain.

The knowledge stabs me like a knife. *She is happy, and I must let her go.* I realize that I must stop trying to make her into the girl she was, now that she is the mermaid she was born to be. As Auntie has said, we must be who we truly are.

The knife plunges deeper as I realize how completely Maren loves O'Neill. Nothing but love could make a person—or a mermaid—glow in such a way. It is the most beautiful and terrible thing I have ever beheld. Beautiful, as all true love is. Terrible, because the thing I feel for O'Neill is paltry, dull, and silly in comparison.

From this moment on, I swear to banish my unsisterly feelings for O'Neill. It is a hollow promise I make to myself, one that I fear I shall break a thousand times before learning how to keep it.

I will do my best to let go of both of them: the mermaid and her true love. They will be who *they* must be. Who am I to interfere with that?

I pity him, truly I do. His time with her is short. For what place could there be in the ocean for a human peddler boy—other than as food for a shark. Heaven forbid such a thing!

O'Neill nudges me. "What is it?"

"Nothing," I lie. He must arrive at his moment of truth and surrender on his own. I have known him since we were infants, and I know he would not accept such a painful truth from me. His bright, unquenchable hopefulness is one of the things that makes him who he is. One of the things that makes me—*made* me—love him. Only brutal experience and unchangeable, visible facts could ever make him give up on making Maren human again.

When Maren reaches her ocean home and leaves him on the shore, what will become of him?

A spring snowstorm shuts us all inside the cozy cottage. The fire blazes as the wind howls and O'Neill sings a naughty sea chantey that makes even our mermaid blush.

"Kraa," says Pilsner, shaking his head in what I take to be approval of the unsavory lyrics. The impish bird perches at the foot of Maren's tub and preens his blue-black plumage.

"Enough of the wholesome entertainment," Scarff says, setting his pennywhistle aside and scratching Osbert behind the ears. "I owe you children the rest of the tale I began a few days ago."

We pull our chairs closer to Maren, forming a semicircle around the tub. Maren snatches O'Neill's hand and bats her shimmering eyelashes. The mermaid version of my sister is even more flirtatious than the human girl was. Then again, no village lad could hope to compare to our O'Neill.

"Where were we? Boston, was it? Just off the ship, trying to get our land legs back. Yes, that was where we left off. So, Verity and I set out upon the road, living much as we had back in the Old Country. A penny here, a fresh loaf there . . . but the cold in America proved much more biting than any we had known before. As luck would have it, we met up with a little old man by the name of Willie Brady. A traveling tinker he was, bereft because his partner had recently succumbed to consumption. At the end of his rope, he said he was, about to dig a hole and bury himself if only he could figure out how. But didn't our Verity talk sense into Willie Brady? And in two shakes of a lamb's tail, we were on the road together, selling pots and pans and spoons and the like, as well as Verity's cough elixirs and headache powders. A grand time it was! At night we'd light a nice fire in the caravan's little potbelly stove and we'd bed down as warm as fleas on a spaniel."

"Willie Brady was like a father to us. A kinder man you'll never meet," Auntie adds.

"Come spring, we rolled into Pennsylvania. Or, rather, we bumped and bounced. The roads were terrible then, and only got worse with the thaw. The mud would swallow your shoes whole and never give them back. One day, that evil mud took hold of Brady's favorite horse's leg and snapped it like kindling. How he wept over that horse! The loss of her broke his heart, and he dwindled down to a bone and a hank of hair after that. On Midsummer's

Eve, he breathed his last. We buried him at twilight, at the edge of a field flashing with fireflies."

Maren sighs and slips a bit further into the water, taking O'Neill's hand with her. His sleeve wicks water up to his elbow, but he does not complain.

Scarff coughs into his handkerchief. "Yes, I miss the old fellow to this day. Lucky, he was. I am certain of that, for after he died, *bad* luck took hold of us without delay. Less than twenty miles from here it happened. And Verity has never been able to set foot off this mountain since." He is overcome by a fit of coughing.

Auntie passes him a green bottle. "Time for your medicine, dear," she says. "I will finish this story, if you please."

Scarff nods in assent and gulps down the dark liquid.

"We came into Yardley Corner, a tiny town at the base of Llanfair Mountain. Not a trace of it remains today. The forest has reclaimed every inch of soil and stone. Well, in this town there lived a half-faerie woman, two hundred years old or more. She recognized me on sight as one of her kind, and she hated me for it. No matter that we were only passing through, only selling cough elixir and sewing needles and such. I discerned, by the atmosphere about her, that she possessed proficiency in the Dark Arts—potent black magic that Albruna had forbidden me to learn. This witch woman took it into her mind that I was her greatest enemy, trespassing on her territory. She was the healer on this mountain, she said, but if I wanted her place, I could have it. I wanted to settle there as much as I wanted to grow a third arm, and I told her so. She called me a liar and before I knew what was happening, she threw a powerful hex powder over me and Scarff, saying, 'To this mountain you are bound, Verity Half-Fey, never to leave it till Death claims you. And from this mountain you are banned, Ezra Scarff, but for thirteen days a year, until the dark horse and raven return, and the three rubies of the gypsy king fall into your wife's hand, and your last golden hair turns as silver as the moon.' She thought she was being quite generous giving us thirteen days a year together, the hag."

"Zedekiah and Pilsner," I say. "The dark horse and raven. And you have the rubies, Auntie?"

She reaches into her pocket and brings forth a velvet box. "They're here. The gypsy king himself gave them to Scarff. Said he'd been told to do so in a dream."

"And Scarff's winter fever turned his last golden hair silver," O'Neill says. "How many years has it been since the hex bound you?"

Auntie caresses Scarff's bearded cheek. "We lost count long ago. What does it matter? We are together now."

"And I may come and go as I please," Scarff says. "Not that I plan to leave my bride anytime soon. Indeed, I do believe I will choose to go only as far as bed." He coughs again.

"Indeed," Auntie says. "Come along now. You'll find my bed a hundred times more comfortable than that lumpy old mattress you keep in the caravan."

"Nonsense, woman," Scarff grumbles. "That mattress was good enough for Willie Brady, and it's good enough for me." He laughs and coughs at the same time as Auntie wraps an arm about his shoulders and steers him toward her bedroom.

"Don't stay up too late, dears," Auntie calls back to us.

Of course, Maren is already asleep. Lately, she sleeps most of the day away, and all of the night. I miss her.

Quietly, with practiced ease, O'Neill and I refresh the tub's water. And as I put another log on the fire, he unrolls his blankets along the far wall of the kitchen, as far away from Maren as he could get without going outdoors. Osbert scampers to his side and turns about three times before settling down with his barbed tail over O'Neill's legs and his snout upon O'Neill's chest.

"Good night," O'Neill and I whisper.

I crawl into the bed Maren and I used to share. The chilly sheets make me shiver. It occurs to me that I am the only one sleeping alone, for Pilsner perches beside Maren, Auntie and Scarff are snuggled up in the next room, and O'Neill and Osbert are cuddling in the kitchen.

I wonder if I should ask Zedekiah to keep me company, but remember that O'Neill called the horse a blanket hog. And on such a frigid night, I'd rather keep my blankets.

CHAPTER TWELVE

It is two days after Easter. O'Neill grips the reins as the colorful caravan jostles down the hole-pocked road toward Llanfair Village. Every bump knocks my shoulder against his and causes my pencil to jump. "This list will be completely unreadable," I say.

"Did you put down salt? We will need a lot of it to keep our mermaid happy on our travels." O'Neill grips the reins more tightly as the caravan rolls over a series of potholes. "Easy, Job! Easy, January!" He shouts to be heard above the din of wind chimes and pots and pans colliding as they swing from their hooks beneath the eaves.

"Salt, yes. Do you think ten pounds is enough? Perhaps I should buy twenty. Or thirty."

"And I promised Osbert a sack of licorice lozenges," O'Neill says guiltily.

"Good heavens, O'Neill! That wyvern needs licorice like he needs another tail! It makes him giddy, you know. You'll be forced to play fetch-the-stick with him for a full day and night after he gulps it down."

"Spoken like a true wyvern's mother." His lopsided smile appears. I must remind myself that he is nothing more than my almost-brother, no matter how handsome he might be.

"This from the young man who snuggles up with the wyvern each night. Will you two be getting married this June, by any chance?"

He jabs his elbow into my arm. "If you were a boy, I'd fight you for such an insult."

"To defend your beloved wyvern's honor?"

"You have wounded me!" He clutches his chest. The horses mistake his tugging of the reins for a command, and they slow down. "Trot, my beauties," he calls to them. "Now back to the list. It's a long journey we're in for—we must not forget anything. Let's think on it."

After a few minutes, I lose focus on the list and begin to worry. When I can contain my anxieties no longer, I ask, "How long will it take to reach the ocean?"

"Two or three weeks, depending on the roads and the weather."

"I hope Maren will last that long. She is so small now that she can almost swim in the bathtub," I say. I pick a pine needle from my skirt and toss it to the wind.

"Job and January will do their best to carry us there speedily. They have sworn a solemn oath to me." The horses whinny as if in agreement. O'Neill winks at me like a storybook scoundrel.

"Can you not be serious for five minutes, O'Neill?" Suddenly, I am weary to the soul.

"You think I am teasing? You don't believe that animals communicate with me?" he asks, sullen.

"Of course I do. I *know* they do. That is not the issue. What drives me mad is that you carry on playing and winking when the situation calls for solemnity."

He fumbles with his cuff. I know that even despite my tirade he is itching to do some parlor trick to lighten my mood. "I swear,

O'Neill, if you pull a flower from your sleeve, I will jump off this wagon," I say.

"Sorry," he replies sadly.

I have hurt him, and I deeply regret it. "No, I am sorry." I touch his arm and he winces.

"Perhaps I should take Maren to the ocean alone, then, if you cannot tolerate me. If you believe I am nothing but tricks and amusements without substance."

"O'Neill, please forgive me," I beg. "You know that you are my dearest friend. And I do love your tricks and illusions. It is just that I am so tired and confused. The world is not at all what I thought it was. There is more magic in it, and more mystery, and more pain."

He lets the reins slacken in his hands and turns his face to me. A smile lurks at the edges of his mouth. "I forgive you, Clara dear. And I hope that you will soon see that the world is also more beautiful than you had known, and more full of kindness and love. Perhaps, on our journey, you will find this out for yourself. You will come with Maren and me, won't you?"

"Yes," I say. "If you left me behind, I would send my dangerous wyvern after you. He would eat you for supper and bring me back your boots as a souvenir." My humor has returned, much to my surprise.

"Ah," he says, shaking the reins to hurry the horses now that we've reached level ground, "I am afraid you actually mean that."

"Never cross a wyvern," I say. "And never, ever cross one of Verity's daughters."

"Wise advice," he says with that crooked O'Neill grin, the one that brings the sunshine out from behind a clouded heart. The one, I must remind myself, that belongs to my sister's true love. But as the proverb goes, even a cat may look at a king.

As O'Neill hitches the horses to the post in front of Norton's Feed Store, Mrs. Locke and Mrs. Grieg take notice of the caravan and scurry across the street, waving and yoo-hooing. As Scarff and O'Neill are wont to brag, such middle-aged housewives find their exotic wares irresistible.

With the charisma of a stage actor and the skill of an experienced vendor, O'Neill throws open the doors and cabinets of the colorful wagon and begins to expound upon the incomparability of his merchandise. He is a whirlwind of charm and flurrying silk scarves, trays of silver rings and boxes of Chinese fans.

List in hand, I leave O'Neill to his work and seek out Mr. Peterman at the general store.

While Mr. Peterman gathers the items we need, I wander about the store, hoping that browsing might help me remember anything I forgot to put on the list.

"Hello, Miss Clara," Simon's voice says from behind me.

I turn to him. "Good morning, Simon," I say. "You are looking well."

"I was married last Saturday," he says. "Do you remember Tabitha Gorse?"

"Yes," I say. "She moved to Iowa a few years ago, didn't she?"

"She moved back here in February," he says. He shifts his weight from one foot to the other nervously. He clears his throat twice, then asks, "How is your sister?"

"Very changed, I am afraid."

"I'm sorry," he says. "Truly sorry." Is that a tear in his eye or a trick of the light? He turns away from me and takes a few slow steps.

"She liked your Christmas gift," I say. "The pretty stone you sent. She keeps it in her locket, so it is always with her." I do not know if it was proper or kind for me to say so, but he looks back at me for a moment and almost smiles.

"Good-bye," he says. He leaves the store quickly, without purchasing a thing. I think he loves Maren still. I feel sorry for his wife.

"Your order is ready," Mr. Peterman announces. "I'll carry it out for you. All that salt makes for a heavy load. It's an odd time of year to be pickling and preserving, isn't it?"

I hold the door for him. "You know Auntie and her strange concoctions," I say.

I am glad we will leave Llanfair Mountain soon. Hiding a mermaid is proving more difficult than hiding a hundred-pound pet wyvern.

We reveal our plans to Scarff and Auntie during our habitual evening gathering in front of the fireplace.

"You must let me come," Scarff says. "I insist upon it."

"No, dear," Auntie says. "The children are right. You are not well enough for such a journey. Besides, I have not been left alone in over seventeen years. It is your spousal duty to stay with me." She pats his arm. "This is their journey to take. They are young and strong, and clever, as well. They are fit for travel and adventure, unlike us. Although it pains me to think I will not see Maren enter her new home."

Scarff grumbles under his breath, but argues no more.

"We will leave in two days," O'Neill says. "I will make sure the caravan is in good repair. Clara has been gathering supplies, and Maren is quite ready to go."

In fact, Maren's face is radiant with expectation. She wriggles her tail and slides down into the water, submerging herself completely. Smiling, she blows a string of tiny bubbles and watches them pop above her.

From head to tail fin, I doubt she measures more than four feet now.

"We bought a washtub to carry Maren," I say. "It should be quite comfortable."

"You must avoid the trains at all cost," Scarff says. "I do not trust the iron beasts."

"We would not risk taking a train," O'Neill says. "Can you imagine us *not* being noticed transporting a mermaid in a tub of water?"

Scarff grunts and folds his arms across his chest.

Auntie shakes her head sadly. "How I hate to lose my seashell girl," she says. "But if anyone in the world is happy, it is Maren as a mermaid."

Tears stick in Scarff's beard like drops of dew on tangled grass. Auntie grips his shoulder and says, "Come to bed, dearest. It's time to put our cares to rest for the day."

Auntie and Scarff lean over the tub and Maren comes out from beneath the water, offering her sparkling cheek for good night kisses. As the couple disappears into their bedroom, Maren beckons to O'Neill. She gestures that she wants to hold his hand, and that she wants him to sing for her.

He pulls a chair in close to the tub and does as the mermaid demands.

Discomfited by the intimacy between them, I collect teacups and saucers and take them to the basin of sudsy water Auntie left heating on the side of the stove. Even with my back to them, I feel like an intruder.

O'Neill sings softly:

On the wings of the wind, o'er the dark rolling deep,
Angels are coming to watch o'er thy sleep.
Angels are coming to watch over thee
So list to the wind coming over the sea.

Hear the wind blow love, hear the wind blow.

Lean your head over and hear the wind blow.

Oh, winds of the night, may your fury be crossed;
May no one who's dear to our island be lost.
Blow the winds gently, calm be the foam,
Shine the light brightly and guide them back home

Hear the wind blow love, hear the wind blow.
Lean your head over and hear the wind blow.

My hands forget their task. Never has his voice sounded so beautiful. Every note carries unconstrained love up from the depths of his soul.

Something catches my eye and I turn. There, at the window, is the unmistakable face of Simon Shumsky. He stares at Maren and O'Neill, not noticing me at all. He sees what I now see: the clasped hands of lovers, O'Neill's blond head resting against the top of Maren's coppery hair. And the swishing of Maren's mermaid tail above the water's surface.

"O'Neill," I cry, knowing it is too late.

A second later, Simon is gone.

If wishing could get me anything, I would wish that I had remembered to close the curtains after I'd hung them, freshly laundered, that morning. I would wish that Osbert—lying by the cellar door, dead to the world due to the strong medicine Auntie has prescribed for his spring cold—had alerted us to the unwelcome guest.

And as much as I like Simon Shumsky, I would wish him to the moon.

Chapter Thirteen

The sun is rising, an orange ball of flame peeking over the next mountain. We have not slept a wink, O'Neill and I. Instead, we spent the night frantically packing and arranging, gathering maps and clothes and food. For we must leave the mountain immediately, before Simon has a chance to spread the news of Maren's change.

Once we are gone from the mountain, Scarff will make it known in the village that O'Neill, Maren, and I have gone to visit far-off relations. Scarff is able to speak falsely for our protection even if Auntie cannot.

And Simon will likely be labeled "touched in the head" if he goes about telling tales of seeing a mermaid in Verity Amsell's kitchen.

Auntie weeps into her handkerchief as Scarff lifts Maren from the bath and lowers her into the washtub. Osbert moans and smacks his tail against the floor like a toddler throwing a fit. Pilsner watches from the mantel, the only calm soul among us.

Scarff and O'Neill pick up the washtub by its handles and carry it to the caravan, sloshing a good third of the water out as they go. Maren grips the sides of the tub to steady herself. She looks like a picture from one of our childhood books, one captioned "An Indian princess travels to her wedding by howdah atop an elephant." Indeed, her face is as bright with bliss as any bride's. She is glad to be going home.

"Promise you'll come back," Auntie says as she embraces me beside the wagon.

"Of course," I say. I swallow hard, willing myself not to cry. I will keep my sadness to myself and not add to the weight of Auntie's sorrow. "Take care of Scarff."

And before our lazy rooster crows, O'Neill is shaking the reins and steering Job and January away from the only home my sister and I have ever known.

I sit inside the caravan beside Maren. Only her head extends above the oilcloth covering the washtub. Scarff tied the cloth down tight before we left—to keep the water and the mermaid from sloshing out. I worry that the rough roads will batter and bruise her. Perhaps we should have brought the bathtub; it would have given her more of a watery cushion. It is too late now.

The little window is open so that O'Neill may speak to us from the driver's seat. The clopping of the horses' hooves is barely audible above the sound of the pots, pans, and chimes. I wonder if O'Neill ever tires of those sounds. To me, they have always signaled the approach of joy itself, heralding the arrival of loved ones. What might they mean to me when this journey is finished and I have given Maren over to the tides?

She sleeps, my mermaid sister. Sleeps with a smile on her coral-pink lips, swaying with the motion of the wagon, as if she has not a care in the world. Not one regret, not a single sorrow, not an ounce of pain.

A snort comes from beneath a mound of blankets in the corner. A very familiar snort.

"Osbert!" I scold him as I whisk away his coverings. "You naughty wyvern! You should not have come along!"

Puppylike, he widens his eyes, flattens his ears, and whimpers.

"What is going on back there?" calls O'Neill from the driver's seat. "Is something wrong?"

"That depends on how you feel about stowaway wyverns," I say. And then I notice another creature lurking in another corner. "And stowaway ravens, as well."

"Kraa," Pilsner declares, ruffling his feathers haughtily.

"If you find a small black horse back there, do let me know," O'Neill says, his voice light with laughter.

"As far as I can tell, Zedekiah had the good sense to remain at home." I pat Osbert's scaly head. "What am I to do with you? You must behave yourself, Osbert, and stay hidden. Imagine the trouble you could cause us! All we need is for someone to see you and get a notion to find out what else might be hiding in the caravan!"

Osbert promises to behave with a submissive bow of the head. And then he skulks to Maren's washtub and curls his body about its base. Like the fearsome dragons of old, he is protecting his greatest treasure. I have no doubt that he would give his very life for her. Perhaps it is wise to have him with us.

I sit down again, resting my back against the sumptuous quilts overflowing from the built-in bed. I do not mean to fall asleep, but the rocking of the wagon lulls me into unconsciousness before I have a chance to consider fighting it.

The caravan is still. Mottled sunlight plays upon my closed eyelids. I listen to the soothing sounds of tinkling glass-and-metal wind chimes, and O'Neill's deep-sleep breathing. For a moment, I am content. All is well here with us: happy mermaid, wyvern sheepdog, sleeping almost-brother, indomitable raven, and girl-brought-by-a-stork.

The prickly surface of Osbert's tongue intrudes upon my peaceful moment, dampening my cheek with slobber. I simultaneously open my eyes and shove him aside. "Get off, you beast," I whisper, trying not to disturb O'Neill and Maren. "You need to go out, do you?"

Wagging his tail, Osbert follows me as I tiptoe through the wagon.

I open the door to a gorgeous scene: Ancient hemlock trees encircle the wagon and tower above me. All the light here is stained green by the passage of sunlight through thick, high branches. Osbert pushes past me and rushes off into the forest as I step down onto a springy brown carpet of little needles.

Job and January stand nearby, unhitched and untethered, with buckets of water and oats at their disposal. They are used to the wandering life and have spent many a night in strange forests and fields. They nod their noble heads in greeting, and I reply in kind.

From here, I cannot see the road. Strangely, although I am surrounded by dancing bits of sunlight, I cannot see beyond a depth of five or six trees. I shiver, no longer so taken with the place. There is magic in this wood, and I am not certain which kind.

"Good morning," O'Neill calls from the doorway. "Lovely place, is it not?" He yawns and stretches before leaping to the ground.

"Are you certain it is safe?" I whisper. "Something about this place makes me uneasy."

"Scarff and I have a pact with the faerie folk of this forest. You are more than safe here."

I am not sure if he is teasing me or telling the truth. Instead of risking hurting his feelings, I do not reply.

He takes a brush from a cubbyhole beneath the wagon and begins to groom the horses. "Shall we cook breakfast, or would you prefer a cold meal and a quick return to the road?"

"We should keep moving," I say without a moment's hesitation. "I'll check on Maren and then slice some bread and cheese."

Osbert bursts out of the blackness, a piece of fabric flapping from his well-toothed jaws. He stops at O'Neill's feet and drops it.

Lifting the wet fabric between two fingers, O'Neill says, "Osbert, what have you been up to?"

The wyvern wags his tail and points with his snout in the direction from which he came.

"What is it?" I ask.

"I believe it is a sample of Simon Shumsky's trouser leg. According to a pair of doves I spoke to last night, he's been following us ever since we left Llanfair Mountain. He must be close now." O'Neill pats Osbert's head. "Good fellow," he says.

"Following us? Why?" Wild thoughts somersault through my mind, visions of Simon taking Maren or killing O'Neill in a jealous rage. But he was always such a kind young man. Perhaps he only wants to find out if what he thought he saw through the window was real.

"Simon has seen a mermaid, and some men cannot stay sane once they do so. Why do you think sailors wreck their vessels chasing after them?"

"He loved her," I say. "He asked her to marry him, and he believed that someday she would consent."

O'Neill's face is grim. "That makes it all the more likely that his mind has turned. He is mermaid-stricken, poor fellow."

"Why are you not afflicted, when you have seen her and touched her and lived with her all these weeks?"

He unbuttons his left cuff and rolls up his sleeve. On his wrist, drawn in ink the color of blood, I see a series of small symbols. "Madame Vadoma gave me this before we left the gypsies' camp," he says. "A tattoo that gives protection against mermaid enchantment."

"Poor Simon," I say, for even as I fear what he might do, I cannot help feeling sorry for him. "Did you know he was recently married?"

"Poor Mrs. Shumsky," O'Neill says. "She is as good as widowed, I am afraid. Simon is beyond all help, even the magic kind. It is a tragedy. But we must not stop here any longer."

Together, O'Neill and I make quick work of hitching the horses to the caravan. Minutes later, we are moving again. Every hoofbeat brings us closer to the ocean. Closer to Maren's home—and farther away from Simon, if we are lucky.

Our next campsite is an abandoned farm.

After thoroughly inspecting the place to ensure that it is indeed abandoned, I throw open the faded red barn doors and O'Neill drives the caravan inside. The back doors of the barn lead to a fenced pasture where tender spring grasses carpet the earth. Job and January are promptly loosed from their harnesses. Whinnying their delight, they frolic in the sunshine like colts before lowering their heads to nibble the green feast laid out before them.

Osbert, too, dances about on his taloned feet. He stretches his wings to their full breadth and sprints into the pasture. As he gains speed, he beats his wings slowly until the wind catches them and lifts him from the ground. He swoops and circles above O'Neill and me, and then dives down to tease me by running the tips of his claws through the top of my hair. He squawks with wyvern joy. After a while, he soars toward the wooded hills in the west and I can see him no more. I hope he has spotted a rabbit or pheasant to chase, and not a mermaid-stricken young husband.

O'Neill brings Maren's tub out of the caravan. She is awake, and she watches him adoringly as he inspects the wagon for any need of repair.

"I'm going to the spring house we passed on the way in," I say, unhooking the buckets from beneath the wagon. "Our mermaid is due for fresh water." *And I am due for time away from young love,* I think.

Maren waves and blows me a kiss before resuming her adoration of O'Neill. I hear him singing as I exit the barn, a Scottish ballad Scarff used to sing after dinner. Those dinners seem a hundred years ago.

"Kraa, kraa!" Pilsner announces that he will accompany me. He flies just ahead of me, as if I might forget the route. I suspect that O'Neill has charged him with protecting me from Simon. I suppose the raven could cause a good deal of harm with claws and beak if he were so inclined.

"Do you miss your home, Pilsner?" I ask. "Do you have a wife somewhere? A nest full of featherless babies?"

Without acknowledging my remarks, he flaps his wings and veers to the east. He perches on the crooked lightning rod, which sticks up from the roof of the farmhouse like the antenna of a wounded insect. From there, he watches me steadily until I return to the camp with buckets sloshing.

After supper (two large trout provided by Osbert, a salad of dressed dandelion greens and fiddlehead ferns provided by O'Neill, and an unfortunate pan of singed biscuits made by me), O'Neill stands and pats his trim belly.

"Ladies, wyvern, and raven," he says with a grand gesture of his arms, "I shall now entertain you as you have never before been entertained."

Maren clasps her hands on her chest. Her sigh sounds like the tiniest of waves caressing the smoothest sand.

"Do excuse me for a few moments while I prepare to dazzle and astound you!" He scampers into the barn, where the caravan is parked.

I add another log to the campfire before sitting on the rickety chair I borrowed from the abandoned house. At suppertime, O'Neill refused the chair I brought him, saying he prefers to have the good earth beneath him. The stains on his trousers attest to this belief.

Maren taps the empty chair with her slim, webbed fingers to get my attention.

"What is it, dear?" I ask.

She makes signs with her hands, touching her heart, forming waves with slow grace, pantomiming the motion of the wagon and the journey of the sun across the sky. I know what she is saying. She says it every day: "Take me to the ocean. How long? How long?" And the question always makes me feel as though I have fallen from a tall tree and hit the ground hard, losing all my breath.

Before I can calculate an answer, O'Neill skips into view. When I see him, I can breathe again. Whenever I see him, I feel rescued somehow.

On his head is a turban of canary-colored silk. His vest, embroidered with strange animals, changes from red to gold and back again as it reflects the firelight. Voluminous sleeves of snow-white cotton are cinched and buttoned at his wrists. I bite my lower lip to keep from laughing at the odd trousers he is wearing: pink silk with green stripes, each absurdly wide leg trimmed with cuffs of silver bells.

"Lady Clara," he says, hands on hips, "do you laugh at me?"

"I am thankful for your bare feet," I manage to say. "For I cannot imagine any shoes that might have complemented such an outfit." I give in to laughter, so overcome that tears spill down my cheeks.

"You dare to mock the coronation garb of Prince Gubabalek of Hubrustan?"

Maren slaps the water with her tail. She, too, is laughing at O'Neill's fashion. Or perhaps the name "Gubabalek."

"Well," he says with a false frown, "since you find my appearance so unsettling, I shall retire for the night. It is plain to me that you do not wish to watch the wondrous feats I meant to show you."

Osbert sneaks up behind him and bestows a sympathetic wet kiss on the back of his neck. And then O'Neill smiles his lopsided smile and begins to pull a handkerchief from a tiny pocket in his vest. He pulls and pulls and pulls, and the handkerchief looks as though it will never end. Finally, ten feet of fabric later, its end emerges. O'Neill uses it to wipe the wyvern spit away.

Maren and I applaud. Osbert, looking pleased that he has lifted O'Neill's spirits, settles down beside Maren's tub to watch the show.

It is an amazing thing to behold.

We have seen many of O'Neill's tricks before: card tricks, flowers pulled from the air, vanishing pocket watches, a dozen eggs pulled from his mouth. We have heard him play the tin whistle and watched him dance the sailor's hornpipe and Irish jig.

But tonight! Tonight he twirls and tosses flaming batons. He juggles four swords at once and then swallows one for good measure. He blindfolds himself and throws knives at a board, making the knives form the letters of Maren's name.

For his final act, he plays the lap harp with his hands and a small drum with his feet while singing a plaintive melody in the gypsies' Romany tongue.

The song ends. I do not clap, finding the sudden silence almost holy.

"Our mermaid is asleep," O'Neill says as he sets his instruments aside.

"Thank you," I say. "You were right that we will not soon forget this night. I am certain that I shall never forget. When I am old, I will think of it as I sit by the fire and knit lumpy stockings for my grandchildren."

He smiles. "The gypsies were kind to me. They treated me as a son, and taught me their arts. You should meet them someday, Madame Vadoma and her family. Each one of them is quite remarkable."

"I would like that very much."

"Come," he says. "Help me get Maren inside. I do not want to splash Prince Gubabalek's finery."

Quietly, we carry the tub to the caravan. Maren remains asleep, only her head and shoulders above the water.

"How happy she looks," I say as I cover the tub with the oil-cloth to trap the warmth. Even a mermaid needs a blanket on a cool spring night. "You make her happy, O'Neill."

He turns away and works at unbuttoning his vest. "It is the least I can do," he says.

Chapter Fourteen

Six days ago, we left Llanfair Mountain. Then, Maren only fit into the washtub while mostly sitting up. Soon, she will be able to fully recline in it. O'Neill says we are making good time, and that we should reach the Atlantic in another eight or nine days. Job and January are swift and nimble creatures, and the weather has been most agreeable.

We camp tonight beside a creek. Osbert patrols the area while O'Neill and I prepare a meal of fresh fish and corn bread. We have placed Maren's tub at the doorway of the caravan so that she might watch the orange and red sunset across the rollicking creek. She sleeps instead.

"I have been thinking," O'Neill says as he places a portion of fish on a stone for Pilsner. "I've been thinking of how we might save her."

I hold out my plate for some fish. "We are saving her now. We are taking her home."

"That is not what I meant, Clara. There must be a way to restore her. To change her back. We should not give up so easily. If the Sea King comes to meet her, we could strike a deal. We could buy her freedom or trade something for the removal of whatever curse is on her. Surely he has the power." His eyes are bright in the firelight, his face aglow with hope and passion. He glances toward Maren's sleeping form. "We must try."

He may be able to resist a mermaid, but he has loved Maren since she was a little girl who could, in the space of an hour, both steal his slingshot and share her cake with him. I reach for his hand. I must begin to speak the truth to him, carefully and slowly, because in little more than a week, he must be prepared to accept it. He must be prepared to give her up. "O'Neill," I say gently. "She does not wish to be saved in such a way. She is happy as a mermaid. She *is* a mermaid."

"That is absurd," he says. He pulls his hand away. "Her happiness is part of the enchantment. Part of the curse that made her into a mermaid. She is blinded by strong magic. You, of all people, should be able to see that."

"Think, O'Neill, of her life. How she has always adored the water."

"I like to swim, and I am no merman." He sets his tin plate on the ground and crosses his arms over his chest. His nose twitches. It is classic angry O'Neill.

"Perhaps you have forgotten this story. One of Auntie's favorites. We were picnicking in the forest, on the big slab of stone we always called the Giants' Dinner Table. Auntie was setting out the food, making everything pretty. Scarff was bouncing you on one knee and me on the other, singing 'Ride a Cock Horse' and carrying on, making us laugh. We children were not quite three years old that summer. After Auntie finished arranging the pickles and tarts and filled the tin cups with milk, she looked about and discovered that Maren was gone. Do you remember where they found her, O'Neill?"

He rubs his twitching nose. "At the Wishing Pool," he says.

"Not just *at* the Wishing Pool. *In* it. Swimming underwater like a minnow. Swimming as if she'd been born a fish and not a girl."

"A natural talent," he says.

"Natural because she is a mermaid."

"You don't want to save her. You, who call yourself her sister. You would just toss her into the sea and be done with her?" His accusations are bitter, but they are entangled with heartache and desperation.

"It is what she wants! What she has always wanted! It is who she is. Who she was born to be, O'Neill. It is her choice, not mine. And not yours."

"I would lay down my life for her! To save her for Auntie and Scarff. To save her for you, Clara. You speak bravely but I know that you could not live without your sister."

I step toward him. I touch his sleeve and speak softly. Perhaps he will hear me yet. "We must let her go, no matter how it pains us. She is happy as a mermaid. It is her desire and her destiny."

"If that is how you feel, then you are as spellbound as she, Clara. But I will find a way to break this magic. I will save her, and you will thank me afterward." He walks away, and the tears I have been withholding spill down my face.

This is my wish: that Maren could speak again—long enough to tell O'Neill the truth that he refuses to hear from me.

I am more than sorry that the truth will break his heart. His brave heart that dares to believe there can yet be a future for him and Maren.

In the morning, O'Neill acts as though we never argued. He sings Maren's favorite sea chanteys at the top of his lungs so she can hear them as the caravan rattles and bumps its way through the woods.

I, for one, am thankful to be under way again, and thankful that Osbert has brought us no more remnants of Simon Shumsky. My hope is that Simon has regained his sanity and gone home to his bride.

When we stop to rest the horses, Pilsner flies off. He does this often of late. No one could blame a strong, young bird for wanting to stretch his fine wings. Sometimes he brings back gifts: a tiny daisy, a plump blackberry, a coin. Once he even brought me an emerald ring, encrusted with dirt. I wear it on my pointer finger and make believe I am a princess on a grand tour of my dominion.

I know I am no princess. I do envy Maren a little, and O'Neill, as well. She is a mermaid; he is a performer. They have their places in the world. Me, I am just a girl who may or may not become a stork. I am not striking to behold and I do not cry pearl tears. I cannot dance or sing or juggle fire. I am a terrible cook and mediocre apothecary—I have seen Auntie dump many of the elixirs I mixed when she thought I was not looking.

On the floor of the caravan, I spy a tiny white feather. Where did that come from? *Is it mine?*

I shiver—and then I pray: *If I must change, let it not happen before we reach the ocean!* For who knows if my transformation would be slow and painful like Maren's, or if I might change from girl to bird in a matter of hours?

Perhaps it is not my feather at all, but an embellishment from a fan or costume. I choose to believe that. I take a deep breath and decide the feather came from O'Neill's wares, not my body.

O'Neill climbs into the wagon and joins Osbert beside Maren's tub. With eyes half-closed, she reaches up, silently asking him to hold her hand. Her hand is no bigger than a baby's now; it does not begin to fill O'Neill's palm. They regard each other tenderly, making secret vows with their eyes.

I turn my back to them and rearrange the jars of spices, trying to imagine the taste of each one to keep my mind from wandering where it should not: along paths of jealousy, sorrow, self-pity, and regret.

A jar of pure white peppercorns reminds me of Maren's mermaid tears. It occurs to me that Maren has not shed a single pearl-tear since we left home. Indeed, why should she cry now? She is on the brink of wonders I will never know, a life beneath the waves with magical creatures. And meanwhile, she has O'Neill's devotion.

"We must stop for supplies at the next town," O'Neill says behind me.

"Yes," I say. I place the jar of peppercorns into the rack. "There is not enough salt left to keep Maren supplied for another day, and we are almost out of cheese. Pilsner gobbles it down as if he is near starvation, despite his many foraging trips."

"Onward we must go, then," he says. I listen to the faint sloshing of water and imagine Maren embracing him by way of farewell. Only after I hear the sound of his footsteps behind me do I turn to face him.

"Pilsner has not come back," I say.

"He will find us. He always does," O'Neill says. He rubs my shoulder. "No need to worry, my dear."

"My, you remind me of Scarff sometimes." I smile, thinking fondly of the man who has always been like a father to me, in spite of his lengthy absences.

"That is a grand compliment," O'Neill says. Quick as lightning, he kisses my cheek. "Settle in now. I'll let Job and January know their rest is done." He leaps out the back door, turning a somersault in the air and landing on his feet so nimbly that no dust is stirred.

Weak in the knees, I sit on the edge of the bed. My skin burns where his lips touched it. My heart turns over like a thirsty leaf in the presence of a cloud full of rain.

For the next half hour, I berate myself for the renewed unsisterly feelings I have for my almost-brother. They are his fault this time, not mine.

Leaning over to reach the dresser, I pick up a gilt-framed hand mirror and examine my face. It is still ordinary. His kiss left no mark on my skin. If only it had not left a mark on my heart.

I should be angry with him. To kiss me seconds after embracing my sister! It is obscene. It is cruel. But then again—had I not just compared him to Scarff? Has Scarff not given me many such fatherly kisses on that very cheek? Surely O'Neill meant his kiss to be like Scarff's: sweet and chaste. Of course that is how he meant it.

How often must I remind myself that he has chosen Maren and not me? How often must I remind myself to rein in my ridiculous emotions?

I force myself to look long at Maren.

Although she is no longer than O'Neill's arm, she is beautiful. Her skin has the sheen of a perfect pearl, pale and smooth and bright. It sparkles as if dusted with crushed diamonds, even in the dimness of the caravan, around her closed eyes and along her delicate cheekbones. The gold locket resting on her chest looks dull, she so outshines it. The iridescent scales, which begin just below her navel, glisten like thin slices of rare gems laid in row after row down the length of her. And where her dainty feet used to be, a glorious fan of silvery green tail. Every inch of her is stunningly beautiful. Indeed, it is the very beauty sailors would gladly die in pursuit of.

Somewhere inside this enchanting splendor, my sister still lives. The one who has heard my secrets and seen my midnight tears. The one who can name every scar on my body (and who caused a few of them herself). The one who has been with me since my first October, who has loved me as I have loved her. We meant to grow old together; we made promises for the future that will not be kept.

This girl, my sister, Maren, loves O'Neill, I remind myself solemnly. And once more I put away my feelings for him. I beg the stars above (though they cower behind daytime clouds) that he will not kiss me again. Ever.

"Are you asleep, Clara?" O'Neill calls from outside. "The store will close soon."

I am surprised to find the wagon still. "I'm coming," I say. I pull the oilcloth up to cover Maren, leaving only her small, doll-like head visible. "Osbert, you have guard duty," I tell him firmly. "Be good and I'll bring you some licorice."

He wraps his barbed tail snugly around the tub, and without a sound swears to protect his mistress.

With furrowed brow, O'Neill glares at the map. "Did we turn right at Fulton Mills, or did we turn left?"

"I do not recall," I say, offering January a carrot. We have stopped to rest the horses in a grove of blossoming fruit trees, hiding our wagon in the midst of row after row of gloriously scented branches. A fine place to be if one must lose one's way—but I will not say so to O'Neill and risk offending him.

He shakes the map and groans. He rakes a hand through his blond hair several times. "This could cost us another day. How could I have taken a wrong turn when every minute counts?"

"You are tired," I say soothingly. "We are all tired. Everyone makes mistakes when they are tired."

"If we don't make it in time . . . If she shrinks away to nothing before we reach the ocean, I will never forgive myself."

Job takes a carrot from my hand and whinnies his thanks. I face O'Neill and say with conviction, "We will make it."

"So *now* you believe in me?" A pitiful half smile accompanies his question.

"I have always believed in you, O'Neill. I have known you were the heroic type since you rescued me from the top of Auntie's tallest oak tree, when we were both five years old."

"Ah, yes. Maren dared you to climb higher than the barn roof, and you scrambled up the tree like a squirrel."

"I wanted to prove that I was as brave as both of you were. I didn't let myself think before I climbed up—and then I looked down," I say.

"You froze. Even from the ground, I could see that you'd gone as pale as a ghost. I scampered up after you and spent the next two hours talking you down, branch by branch."

"I was not brave at all. I am still not brave. Thank goodness *you* are here to help us, now that we are two damsels in distress."

He reaches out and runs his fingers lightly across my cheek. "You are no damsel in distress, Clara. You are far braver than you think. You left your comfortable home behind to venture through thick forests and over terrible roads so that your sister might have a chance to live. And Maren and I could not have made this journey without you. I would not have taken care of her half as well as you have. I would have oversalted her water and never remembered to wash her face at night. I would have overslept every day, forgotten to eat, and made a hundred more wrong turns. So you see? You are utterly indispensable."

I step backward, my face aflame. "Yes. Well. We ought to resume the journey before night falls." I refuse to meet his gaze. Must he touch me? My chest aches inside with confusion and longing and hopelessness.

"There—I even need you to remind me to focus on the task at hand," he says. "I'd be hopeless without you."

"I will check on Maren while you ready the horses." I rush into the caravan, heart pounding rebelliously. *I am not so brave,* I think. *And I am far from indispensable. Foolish, yes. A traitor to my beloved sister and her true love, yes. But not brave.*

CHAPTER FIFTEEN

I hear a mighty crack—the sound of a cut tree splintering just before it falls—and the wagon lurches and leans. "Whoa," O'Neill shouts, "whoa, there!"

Trinkets and boxed goods tumble from the shelves as the caravan comes to a quick stop. Water splashes out of Maren's washtub and drenches Osbert. The mermaid's eyes widen with fear and she desperately grips the tub's sides. "Are you hurt?" I ask.

She shakes her head. Her coral-pink lips form the question, "What happened?"

"I will find out," I say. I hurry to put on my shoes and meet O'Neill outside.

"A broken wheel," he grumbles. He stares at the fractured yellow spokes and torn metal. He utters a few words I do not recognize. From his mood and tone, I guess that they are the expletives of a foreign tongue. "I have never seen one quite so destroyed. We are miles from the next town, and from the look of those clouds, I'd say we are in for quite a storm within the hour."

"We will camp here for the night, then," I say, attempting to sound cheerful. "I will lay out a picnic in the caravan. Like when we were younger and pretending to travel to forbidden kingdoms."

"For all your talk of playing, Clara, I see the worry in your eyes." He takes a deep breath and releases it slowly. "But you are right. Nothing can be done tonight. I will unhitch Job and January and find them a place to graze, and then I will join you."

Of all the traditions of our shared childhood, the caravan picnic has always been a favorite. So, despite the bothersome delay the wheel causes, I prepare our meal with gratitude. I will take joy in keeping this custom with my sister—one last time before she leaves the land.

From Scarff and O'Neill's many trunks and drawers, I choose a pink damask tablecloth and richly painted Turkish dishes, a wooden cutting board in the shape of an elephant, goblets of ruby glass, and a knife with the bust of a Roman god for a handle. I set three places, just like always. I arrange pillows and cushions for O'Neill and me to sit upon and clear a place for Maren's tub.

It is not a royal banquet by any measure: hard cheese, two-day-old bread, lukewarm cider, and pickles. Lighting the caravan stove to cook bacon or boil water for tea would only raise the temperature inside from sultry to oppressive. We have none of Auntie's jams or cakes, no sliced cold chicken or clove-scented ham. But in the golden lamplight, with the low rumble of thunder in the distance, it seems a fine feast.

All is ready. I wait for O'Neill, feeling the flutter of butterflies in my stomach, as if he has been gone all winter and is about to come home again—*to me*. I wish I had changed my dress and tidied my hair, but I hear his boots on the steps and it is too late for fussing.

Little raindrops glisten in his golden hair. His somber expression melts away as he beholds the arrangement of plain food and exotic tableware. "You are an artist," he says. "I should paint it rather than eating it."

"Nonsense," I say. "Will you bring Maren's tub to her place? Even though she cannot eat, she would hate to miss a caravan picnic."

"Of course," he says.

After O'Neill sets Maren's washtub down, he settles among the cushions. For a moment, he is the picture of relaxation. But then our mermaid awakens and signs her demand: O'Neill must move closer to her so that she may hold his hand. He obeys.

I pour cider into the goblets and pass one to O'Neill.

"Let us pretend," he says. "Let us make believe that the caravan is parked in front of Auntie's cottage. We have spent the day exploring the mountainside, getting scratched by thornbushes and eating wild blackberries. We have held wriggling red salamanders in our hands and watched baby birds learn to fly. We have seen strange flowers growing along rushing streams, and we have walked barefoot over spongy moss. Now we are tired and happy and hungry, and this is the best of suppers in the best of places."

"Yes," I say. "And after our meal, you will tell us of your travels and show us some special treasure you found on a riverbank or in an abandoned tent."

Lightning flashes. Thunder shakes the wagon. Osbert whimpers and begins to pace. Storms make him uneasy, and he has no cellar to retreat to here.

"Sit, Osbert," O'Neill says gently. "It is just a little storm."

"Perhaps he needs to go out," I say. I do not intend to let a silly wyvern ruin my picnic.

Half flying and half running, Osbert dashes out the door as soon as O'Neill opens it. "I guess you were right," he says, going to close the windows as the rain begins to lash at the wagon.

The wind makes the caravan creak and sway on its axles as the storm grows fiercer. But we are in our own little world. Maren naps again, and O'Neill and I eat all the pickles and drink all the cider. We are beyond full when O'Neill pulls a tin of shortbread biscuits out of a drawer—yet we devour them all. We take turns reminding each other of the events of our childhood, and we laugh until our bellies ache.

"It's late," O'Neill says. He begins to gather dishes and jars. "Let's set these things aside to make room for your cot and deal with them in the morning."

I yawn. "That is a fine idea," I say. I reach for his goblet, and my hand brushes against his. Both of us freeze. For a moment, our eyes meet. *I could die happy right now,* I think. He opens his mouth to speak, and a strange sound somewhere between a cough and a hiss comes from behind him.

I pull my hand away. Maren is glaring at me, her ocean-colored eyes dark with anger. "Forgive me," I say to O'Neill. "How clumsy I am."

"Do not mention it," he says. His face is flushed with embarrassment—a rare thing for our worldly peddler boy. "I will venture out to see how Job and January are faring."

He leaves me alone with Maren. "You do not need to be jealous," I say. "I know how you feel about him, sister. And you would have to be blind not to see how he favors you."

She slaps her tail against the water and pouts. I will say no more to her tonight. There will be no pleasing her.

Something is very wrong.

Coughing and choking, I force my eyelids to open.

The air swirls with thick smoke and orange and yellow flashes, like a lightning-filled thundercloud is somehow trapped within the caravan.

The caravan is on fire. Tongues of flame dance across the tapestried bed. Scarff's treasures ignite one after the other, the fire roaring its delight as it consumes more and more of them.

Lungs burning, I crawl toward the place where Maren's tub usually sits. I call her name, but my voice comes out in a weak croak.

"Is anyone in there?" a stranger's voice calls as the door is flung open. The flames jump with joy at the influx of air.

"Yes," I answer feebly. Seconds later, strong arms lift me and carry me through the smoke and flames to safety. "Two more," I say to the man as he lowers me to the ground.

The man bounds back into the wagon and emerges with O'Neill slung over his shoulder. O'Neill's clothes are singed and his head lolls against the rescuer's shoulder blade.

I grab the man's arm as he sets O'Neill beside me. "My sister. In a washtub," I say between coughs.

"There is no one else," he says.

Flames shoot into the sky above the wagon. Bottles tinkle and pop as they explode. The bright paint blackens and flakes off into the night.

I will find Maren, I tell myself. I try to stand, but the smoke has weakened me. I crumple to the dirt as the blazing caravan collapses into an unrecognizable heap.

"Poor dears! Such a tragedy!" a woman says. Her voice is lyrical and strangely accented. "Bring them to our camp, Jasper. I will see to their wounds."

"Maren," I whisper. My throat feels seared. "My sister."

The woman bends over me. She is veiled in red-and-purple silk, and her skin is the color of caramel. "Do not speak. The smoke is in your throat. I will get it out, and then you may tell us your story."

"My sister," I whisper again. "In the washtub."

The woman stands. "Jasper?"

"I checked, Mama. Three times. She's gone."

"That cannot be! You must find her. Look there—I see footprints in the dirt. The footprints of a big man. Follow them!"

The rescuer, Jasper, runs.

My chest tightens with fear.

Maren is gone. Taken.

By Simon? Did Simon set the caravan ablaze?

I try to sit up but fail.

The woman says, "Rest here. I will bring you water and blankets. When my son returns, he will take you to our tents and we will make you more comfortable, poor lamb."

Only then do I remember Pilsner. I pray that he managed to escape.

What of Job and January, left to graze nearby?

And where is Osbert? He never returned after he ran off panicking in the storm.

Have I lost my most dear, nonhuman companions, *and* my sister, in one night?

Beside me, O'Neill stirs. "Clara?"

"I am here," I whisper. I find his hand and grasp it. He squeezes my fingers tightly, with the grip of someone in great pain.

I turn my head toward him. The moonlight shows me his soot-covered profile. A thin strip of whiteness runs from the corner of his eye to the lobe of his ear, marking the trail of his tears. I want to cry out for the woman to return, to beg her to bring something to ease his suffering, but I am overcome by another fit of coughing.

As my coughing lessens, O'Neill's hand relaxes in mine. He is either asleep or unconscious, in a temporary escape from pain. Auntie would say that it is a good thing, that a mind at rest frees the body to work at healing itself.

But is there anything in the world that will heal his heart once he hears that Maren is gone?

CHAPTER SIXTEEN

I am lying on a cot inside a large tent. I vaguely remember the man called Jasper carrying me to this place, his mother covering me with soft blankets and holding a cup of water to my parched lips before I fainted or fell asleep.

Now fully aware, I look about the tent. It is furnished as colorfully and splendidly as the caravan was, with copper lanterns, embroidered cushions, and trunks full of unknown treasures—like an illustration from the tale of Aladdin. But this place lacks Scarff's warmth and O'Neill's charm, the very things that made their wheeled home a place of delight rather than a mere collection of fripperies.

The image of the caravan reduced to smoldering ashes floats before me like some horrific ghost. I wish it were nothing but the memory of a nightmare, to be easily dismissed and forgotten.

A string of little bells tinkles as the door flap is pushed aside and Jasper's mother enters.

She sits down on the edge of the cot and hands me a mug of fragrant tea. "Your sister is a mermaid," she says without wonder, as if having a mermaid in one's family is commonplace. "She is very beautiful."

"You found her?" I almost drop the tea.

"My son Jasper found her, and the man who took her, a few miles from here. I am afraid that it did not end well for the thief."

"Simon," I say. "He followed us."

"He will follow you no more. The path of his life ended in misfortune." The woman pours red syrup from a bottle into a spoon. "For your throat and lungs," she says.

I swallow the medicine. It tastes like spoiled potatoes and overripe cherries with a dash of coal dust. I rinse it down with half the tea. "Is my sister all right?"

"She is very weak, but I have seen to her. I have dealt with her kind before, and I know what they must have, what elements will keep them alive outside the sea."

"Thank you," I say, although I care for neither her choice of words nor the coolness of her tone.

"She is not your true sister, the mermaid," she says, laying a palm against my forehead to check for fever.

"Not my sister by blood, but every bit the sister of my heart."

"Ah," she says, "a sister is more valuable than rubies." A dozen gold bracelets clink together on her arm as she lifts her hand from my forehead. "No fever. Good."

"How is my friend? The young man?" I am very anxious to hear of O'Neill *and* to change the subject.

"Neelo sends his greetings. He is much improved, but his legs were badly burned and will take time to grow strong again. He rests in Jasper's tent."

"O'Neill," I say. I feel a weight lift from my heart; Maren and O'Neill are safe.

"He tells me you are called Clara. My name is Soraya. Soraya Phipps. My son Jasper rescued you and your friends, and later you will meet his father, the great Dr. Phipps."

"How fortunate that you found us," I say.

"Yes," she says. "It was most fortunate."

"When can I see my sister?"

"Soon. It is best not to disturb her for a day or two as she acclimates to her new habitat."

Something about the word *habitat* does not sit well with me. But perhaps Soraya chose the only English word she knew to describe Maren's liquid-filled home. The strength of her accent makes it plain that English is not her native tongue.

"Maren needs to go to the ocean soon, or she will die," I say.

"She is fine. We will speak of such things later." Soraya stands. She adjusts her tunic-like dress and the silk whispers like sea on sand, like Maren's voice not so long ago. "Rest now," she says as she brushes the tent flap aside and exits.

My mind is awhirl with the events of the last day (or days—for how am I to know how long I slept?): the wonderful picnic, Scarff's magnificent caravan engulfed in flames, Jasper carrying me to safety, my hand grasping O'Neill's as we lay side by side, Soraya telling me that my sister is safe.

I wonder how Osbert fares, and if anyone will ever tell Simon's widow that he died while attempting to kidnap a mermaid. I doubt she would believe the truth if she heard it.

In a way, Simon sacrificed his life for Maren. And what of O'Neill, who swears to restore her humanness? Will his dedication to his vow cost him his life as well?

I close my eyes and picture Auntie. *"Hush, now,"* I hear her saying. *"Not to worry, my girl. One chicken cannot sit on the whole world's eggs."* I imagine her soft-cotton, plump-armed embrace and her lavender-and-fresh-bread scent, and I am *almost* comforted.

Wishing I were home is as useless as worrying, I suppose. Yet that is my wish.

Chapter Seventeen

Dressed in a borrowed sari and shawl, I step out of the tent into a bright spring morning.

Jasper stands beside the campfire, drinking from a huge mug. He notices me right away and lifts the mug in salutation. "Coffee," he says. "It runs through my veins." He has his mother's lithe figure and dark amber eyes, and his hair is a mop of unruly, brassy curls. He could be twenty or even thirty years old; his boyish face makes guessing difficult. He sets his mug on a chair. "You are Clara," he says. He steps closer and takes my hand, lifting it to his lips. "Your servant, Jasper Armand Phipps."

He presses his mouth against my skin, gazing into my eyes like a dime-novel knave attempting to seduce an innocent maiden. Finally, he releases my hand and says, "Mama has not worn that costume in ages. I must say, it suits you far more than it ever suited her."

The word "costume" unlocks a flood of memories. Where has my mind been? How could I not have recognized these people? How could I have forgotten the medicine show Maren and I attended last spring, and the unsettlingly curious woman who offered to help cure Maren's "condition"? How could I have forgotten Jasper's music and his father's charismatic sales pitch?

"You are quite pale, Clara. Come, sit down." He guides me by the hand to a chair near the fire and takes a seat on a stool beside me. "We must become acquainted."

"Thank you," I say, unable to think of another reply. His suave manner makes me quite uncomfortable. I survey the camp instead of looking him in the eye. I see two tents—one large and one small, both dark-green canvas with red-and-gold pennants flying from their central poles. Between the tents is a mustard-colored wagon (similar in shape to our now-ruined caravan but twice as large). Crimson letters on the side spell out "Dr. Phipps and Company, Medicine Show and Astounding Wonders." A second wagon, its smaller twin, is parked behind the tents.

"Welcome to our nomadic home," Jasper says. "I hope that you have been quite comfortable."

"Yes," I say. "Your mother has been very attentive. But as soon as O'Neill regains his strength, we will leave you. We do not wish to interfere with your routine."

"You are no trouble at all, my dear. I for one find your presence inspiring, the adventure that brought you to us both providential and thrilling. Indeed, I hope you will stay with us long beyond O'Neill's recovery." He lifts my hand from my lap and folds his hands around it. His palms are warm but dry. "I deduce that you carry too many troubles on those pretty shoulders of yours. A bit of fun on the road would put the roses back in your cheeks and boost your sore spirits."

I pull my hand away. Jasper is too charming for anyone's good. "We have travel plans of our own that we must not delay," I say. "But thank you for your kind offer."

"You may yet change your mind." He stands and brushes imaginary dust from his sleeves. "We move on this morning. Tomorrow night, we will perform in the next town. Marsburg, I believe it is called. You will surely be with us that long, at least."

A man steps out of the smaller tent. He is short and stout and dressed in a perfectly tailored gray suit. His shoes are polished so that they reflect the sun. He shakes his silver-tipped walking stick at Jasper. "Son," he says, "quit dallying and begin packing up the tents."

"May I introduce my father, the great Dr. Phipps?" Jasper says. "Papa, this is Clara of the Conflagration."

"Clara," Phipps says. "Pretty enough. I am sure my wife can find a place for you in the show. Do you sing or dance?"

"No, sir," I say. "But we—"

"No matter. Soraya will sort it out." He speaks with authority, as a king who will not be questioned or opposed. "You may go find her now and ask her how you may assist in getting the show on the road, as it were."

"Yes, sir," I say. The doctor's posture tells me it would be futile to disagree.

"Don't just stand there, Jasper. Get to work, lad!" Dr. Phipps saunters toward the wagon, swinging his walking stick as if strolling a city street.

Jasper retrieves his mug and finishes his coffee. "Don't mind the old bear too much. He is always grumpy in the morning." He points toward the farthest tent. "You'll find my mother in that direction, I believe."

"Could I see my sister before we go?" I ask.

"Ah, yes. The mermaid. Mama told me you might inquire of her. She also said you must wait until tomorrow to visit. The mermaid needs time to recover her strength."

"Her name is Maren," I say. "And we have never been apart for more than a few hours. Surely a visit from me would be beneficial." If only I possessed Maren's allure, he would not think of refusing me.

"Jasper!" Dr. Phipps bellows from behind the wagon. "Come here, son!"

Jasper rolls his eyes. "Duty calls. It has been a great pleasure, mademoiselle. We shall meet again." He bows and takes a few steps before turning back to face me again. "A word to the wise, Clara dear: hurry along to Mama and don't get into mischief."

His condescension irks me. I wish my manners did not prevent me from telling him that he is not half as appealing as he seems to believe he is. Instead, I lift the too-long hem of the borrowed sari and walk like a well-mannered young lady in the direction he recommended.

As I pass Jasper's tent, I am tempted to duck inside to visit O'Neill. Feeling disobedient and rather reckless, I give in to temptation and push my way through the tent flap.

"Clara!" O'Neill says, seeing me before I see him. He is cocooned inside a hammock-like bed with only his head and arms free.

"Hush," I say, moving closer so that he might hear my whispers. "I am forbidden to see Maren, and I did not ask permission to see you, so it might be best to keep quiet."

"Why? Have you been causing trouble?"

"You know I have not. But that Dr. Phipps is a fearsome man, and his son is quite . . . perplexing. They visited Llanfair Mountain last spring, selling their sham cures. I do not trust them."

"You worry too much, Clara. They saved us, did they not? Jasper risked his life getting us out of the burning caravan."

"Yes. Well. I would feel much better if I could see Maren, even for a few minutes."

"You will see her soon. And we will return to the road in a day or two at most, whether this Dr. Phipps fellow approves or not. Although I am sorry to tell you we will have to continue without Job and January. Jasper says they fled the fire, but I think they were stolen. They would not have run from me after all our adventures together." He offers me his hand and I notice that his arm is swathed in gauze. "We must not count our losses now, not while Maren still needs our help."

"Are they bad, your injuries?" Against my better judgment, I place my hand in his. My heart beats faster than I wish it would.

"My right leg is the worst. But it should be as good as gold in no time, thanks to Soraya's poultices."

"I am glad you are improving," I say. I try to take my hand back, but his grip is firm. "Please. I should go." I do not add that by holding my hand so sweetly, he makes me betray myself and Maren.

He smiles his crooked smile, his eyes full of O'Neill mischief, and lets go. "As you wish," he says.

I do not say good-bye before scurrying out of the tent, tripping over the sari's hem as I exit.

Such a jumble of feelings crowds my heart again: uncertainty and impatience, love and disgust.

Surely it would be easier to be a stork than a seventeen-year-old girl.

Inside the speeding wagon, O'Neill and I sit on woven mats. Soraya reclines on an upholstered couch, snoring most daintily. Apparently she is unbothered by Dr. Phipps's wild driving, how he relentlessly urges the four horses onward with the crack of his whip and the lash of his tongue.

Following in our dusty wake, Jasper drives the smaller wagon, the one loaded with the doctor's collection of wonders and rarities. According to Dr. Phipps, the mermaid is lucky to be traveling amongst such priceless treasures. I should remind him that she is not an object to be collected, but a beloved sister and friend. Yet I keep silent—out of wisdom or cowardice, or perhaps a bit of both.

Soraya, O'Neill, and I ride in the company of less exalted items. Labeled cases of medicines are neatly stacked along the walls beside trunks of various sizes. Costumes and musical instruments hang from pegs. One shelf holds a row of men's shoes and boots, and another displays a collection of ladies' slippers (some leather, some satin, some spangled with crystals). Boxes and bottles of food crowd a few other shelves. Above my head, a huge burlap bag swings from a hook and rains down grains of rice, one at a time, from a tiny tear in its side.

As rapidly as we cross the countryside, time seems to drag inside the wagon. In my mind, I relive Maren's transformation, from her simple love of water to the first hint of scales upon her side; from discovering her fused-together legs to beholding her brilliant tail fin; from her fading whispers to the sea-on-sand sound of her most recent laughter; from the Wishing Pool to the washtub, and to whatever vessel she now inhabits.

I miss her. I miss her as I'd miss my sight if I were suddenly blind. I miss her as a tree must miss its wealth of leaves come midwinter. I miss her continually, painfully.

Through the open window, I see the shadow of a large bird hover and swoop. *I know that bird*—and it is no bird. It is Osbert! He is safe, and he is with us.

"Worrying again, worry-bird?" O'Neill asks, whispering so as not to disturb Soraya's slumber.

"I've just seen Osbert," I say. "He is following us."

"You see? No real harm can befall us while the wyvern watches. All is well. Other than my leg, that is."

I wonder if Soraya has dosed him with something. How could he believe all is well when Maren is hidden from us and possibly shrinking away?

"We cannot afford to be waylaid," I say. "We do not have time to help put on shows, no matter how beholden we may be to the

Phipps family. We must not continue with them unless they agree to take us to the ocean. Maren's life is in the balance."

"I will ask the doctor," O'Neill says. "He does not frighten me with his shouting and lording."

"Thank you." A pillow tumbles off Soraya's couch and rolls within my reach. I take it and stuff it behind my back. Its softness, combined with Osbert's presence and O'Neill's promise, gives me a measure of comfort.

"I will ask Dr. Phipps's leave for you to see Maren, as well," he says. "I know how much you miss her. All the sparkle has left your eyes."

"Maren is the one who sparkles," I say. I change the subject. "How does it feel to wear such fine clothes?"

O'Neill is dressed in a blue silk shirt and a black vest and trousers pinstriped with yellow. Jasper's garments, obviously.

"As usual, my trousers are two inches too short," he says. "And this shirt smells of Jasper and sandalwood."

"What is it you children whisper of?" Soraya says. Her many bracelets jangle as she yawns and stretches her arms wide.

"We have been friends since we were infants," O'Neill says. "We talk of everything, and sometimes nothing at all."

"Dr. Phipps does not approve of idle talk," Soraya says. "He says that it weakens the soul."

"Then I beg to differ with the doctor," O'Neill says. "I find good conversation very energizing."

"You would do well not to speak to the doctor of your opinions, young man. He does not take kindly to those who oppose him. In Dr. Phipps's show, he is king. He is never wrong."

"Have you never disagreed with your husband?" O'Neill asks.

Soraya's eyes widen in horror. "Never!"

"I see," O'Neill says. He opens his mouth to continue, but I interrupt. I will not sit and watch him endanger himself by picking petty fights with Soraya. If the doctor is king, then she is queen, and O'Neill is dancing on dangerous ground.

"You should rest," I say to him, rather loudly. "You are still recovering from your injuries, after all."

"I *am* tired all of a sudden," he says. Our eyes meet for a moment, and I believe he understands my unspoken plea for him to tread more carefully.

"Sleep," Soraya says. "For how will you repay your debts to us if you do not regain your strength? How much is it worth, the saving of a life? A dozen performances? A whole season's shows? We shall let Dr. Phipps decide, yes?"

I shudder, knowing such a debt can never be repaid. We are butterflies in a net, O'Neill, Maren, and I—and we must find a way to escape while Maren still lives.

CHAPTER EIGHTEEN

The wagon rolls to a stop. Soraya's breaths are deep and even as she indulges in her third nap of the day. Through the window, I see small-town buildings, their windowpanes reflecting the red and purple of the setting sun.

Jasper opens the door and summons O'Neill and me with a gesture. I help O'Neill to his feet and let him lean on me as we make our way through the wagon. With his limping, it is difficult to be quiet—yet we do not wake Soraya.

At the door, Jasper takes over supporting O'Neill, helping him to the ground. "Papa doctor has gone to procure a performance space," Jasper says. "He'll have a drink or two before he comes back. Mama is obviously unconscious. So, now is your golden opportunity to see the mermaid."

"Truly?" I say. "You will take us now?" I could sing for joy at the thought of seeing Maren again.

"This way, lady and gentleman," Jasper says. He leads us to the other wagon. After removing a padlock and chain, he opens the door. "Go ahead, Clara. I will help our gimpy friend."

The wagon is full of wooden boxes and strange shapes draped with lengths of gray cloth. Although the windows are open, the space is dark and dim. The air smells of dust, dried flowers, and old books. We barely have enough room to move among the objects.

Jasper brushes past me and stands beside what appears to be a pillar covered with midnight-blue velvet. He takes hold of one corner of the fabric and pulls it slowly, languidly, as though to build excitement in his little audience. Finally, the velvet slides down to form a dark pool around the base of the largest glass apothecary jar I have ever seen—five feet tall, pale green, and crowned with a fancifully wrought silver lid. "Behold the mermaid!" Jasper says theatrically.

As if on cue, Maren opens her eyes. When she sees me, she presses her doll-sized hand to the glass and smiles. Her color is less ashen—pearlier than when last I saw her. Her skin has regained some of its shimmer. Her copper-gold hair floats about her head like a nimbus.

I kneel beside the jar and place my hand against hers; the layer of glass between us warms slowly. "I have missed you, sister," I say. Although I do not think she can hear me, she smiles wider and blows a kiss with her free hand.

O'Neill lowers himself to the floor beside me. Maren's face lights up, and she flicks her tail prettily. I glance at his odd expression: part fascination, part shock. It is then that I notice she has lost her wrappings and is bare-breasted.

"Good heavens!" I say. "Avert your eyes, O'Neill!"

I do not think he hears me, for he continues staring at her fluttering lashes, flashing scales, and unclothed torso.

Jasper clutches his belly and doubles over with laughter.

"This is not at all amusing," I say, standing in an attempt to block the men's view of my sister.

"You haven't seen much of the world, have you, my dear?" Jasper says.

"What does that matter?" I scramble to throw the velvet cover over the jar. "Morals and manners are not things to be left at home!"

Jasper laughs again, howling like a mad dog. "The mermaid's sister is a *holy* sister!" he blurts once he catches his breath. "And what are you, O'Neill? A priest perhaps?"

The velvet falls over the glass with a whisper.

O'Neill says, "I am sorry, Clara." His face is cherry red.

Jasper smacks his thigh. "What fun we shall have! A straight-laced maiden, an innocent boy in love with a mermaid, and me—bawdy heir apparent to the kingdom of Phipps!"

"This is not amusing," I say again. "Please excuse me. I must find something for my sister to wear." I glare at Jasper until he takes a step back. When he motions for me to pass, I spy the scarlet tattoo on his wrist. The same charm against mermaid enchantment O'Neill wears.

Jasper's mother's words echo in my mind: *"I have dealt with her kind before, and I know what they must have, what elements will keep them alive outside the sea."* Now I am certain that Maren is not the first mermaid to be part of Phipps's vile show. A shiver runs up my spine.

O'Neill follows me outside, limping and grimacing. I turn to chide him as we walk back to the other wagon. "I cannot believe how you stared at her! Scarff would be ashamed of you."

He keeps his eyes trained on the ground. "I am truly sorry," he says. "I behaved like a scoundrel. Will you forgive me?"

"I will try," I say. But he has not just treaded upon my morals; he has also bruised my heart. And bruises do not disappear instantly.

From the other wagon's doorway, Soraya watches us approach, hands on hips. "Where have you naughty children been?" she demands.

Jasper puts an arm around my shoulders, startling me. I had not heard him approach. "They were with me, Mama. No need to worry."

I disagree. We have many reasons to worry, and Jasper and his mother are just two of them.

If I could, I would wish O'Neill's leg healed so that we could take Maren and flee this very hour.

Among the boxes and crates of medicines and soaps, I find a pile of cheaply made scarves. I choose one made of snow-white cambric and bordered with celery-colored lace. I detest stealing even such a little thing, but Maren must be clothed without delay.

The men are busy pitching the tents. Soraya has gone to buy thread. The door to the wagon where Maren is kept stands wide open.

I slip inside unnoticed. A single sunbeam touches the blue velvet covering the glass jar. Is she still alive, I wonder? What if she could wait no longer to go home? My blood runs cold. I force myself to pull the velvet away.

There she is, my sister. She faces away from me, combing her fingers through her bright locks, oblivious to my presence but alive.

I try to lift the ornate lid straight up, but it does not budge. I crack my fingernails and bruise my palms working to unscrew it. And as I am about to give up, the lid turns with a squeak. Three rotations later, I remove it and set it on the floor.

"Maren, come here," I say, peering down into the oily-looking liquid. It smells of cloves and sulfur and honeysuckle, plus a few things I cannot name.

My sister ignores my request. She swims in lazy circles, her silvery green tail undulating and her glossy hair fluttering like a flag in a steady wind. Her bare torso reminds me of a painting of a Greek goddess from one of Auntie's art books. The goddess had the same alabaster skin and round breasts—and seemed just as unbothered by her nakedness as Maren is. But although the goddess was beautiful, she could not compare to Maren. Somehow, despite the incongruity of her womanly mermaid shape and her child-sized body, she is beautiful beyond words.

"Please come here, sister," I say, raising my voice. "Hurry."

She swims to the top of the jar and pokes her head out of the water. When she sees the scarf, she must guess my intent. She pouts and shakes her head.

"Please do this for me," I say. "Even though you are not embarrassed, I am embarrassed for you. Imagine what Auntie would say! After everything she taught us about modesty and virtue."

Maren raises her arms in surrender. I wrap the scarf about her chest and tie it in a double knot at the center of her back. "There," I say. "It is rather fetching, with the lace at the top like that."

She sticks out her tongue like a spoiled child and dives to the bottom of the jar. Her crossed arms and turned back are familiar to me. I have seen both a hundred times during our lifetime of sibling squabbles.

Her sulkiness does not bother me. In fact, it makes me glad. My sister may have a fish's tail, but her independent spirit is the same as it has always been.

"Good-bye, dearest," I say. "I will be back as soon as I can. Osbert is nearby, and so is O'Neill, and we will find a way to take you home soon."

She turns to face me. Bubbles float up from her lips as she mouths, "O'Neill," and presses both hands over her heart. Then she motions again, and I know what she intends to say: *Tell him that I love him.*

"Good-bye," I say again. I crown the jar with its lid and drape the velvet over it.

I will deliver her message to O'Neill. But I wish I did not have to.

CHAPTER NINETEEN

The camp stands like a foreign guest in a dandelion-studded field. The fabric of the two green tents moves in and out with the breeze as if they are breathing. The large wagon is parked in front of them and has been transformed, by the attachment of a raised wooden platform, into a stage complete with red velvet curtains and copper, shell-shaped footlights. Queued in front of the stage, plank benches await the audience.

A big red-and-yellow-striped tent is situated to the right of the stage, a golden pennant snapping on its pole at the peak. The cloth sign above the door proclaims it the "Gallery of Wonders." I have not seen this tent before; Phipps and company must not have pitched it when they visited Llanfair Village.

"Grand, is it not?" Jasper says from behind me, startling me. "It is time for supper, Clara. The townspeople will begin to arrive soon." He wraps his arm around my shoulders and steers me along. "Mama has prepared my favorite dish, in honor of your joining the show."

I try to shrug off his arm, but he fights my efforts. "We do appreciate your kindness, but it is not possible for us to join your show. O'Neill and I must take Maren to the ocean. She will not survive much longer otherwise." Even as the words leave my mouth, I regret them. I ought to have kept silent rather than revealing our plans to leave. I should have waited for O'Neill to speak to Dr. Phipps in his charming, persuasive O'Neill way—although I suspect Phipps will deny his pleas. Why would he give up a prize such as Maren?

"Nonsense," Jasper says. "Maren is fine. The solution Mama concocted for her can keep her healthy for years. I have seen it done."

"It is not what Maren wants, to live in a jar. It is not what is best for her."

"And fretting like a wet hen is not what's best for you, Clara dear. It ruins a girl's looks. Now, relax and breathe in that heavenly aroma," Jasper says, inhaling deeply. "The finest of spices combined to perfection."

We round a corner. Dr. Phipps beckons us to the campfire, where four mismatched wooden chairs and a stool with a tufted cushion have been arranged in a semicircle. O'Neill gives a little wave; I duck out from under Jasper's arm and hurry to sit beside him.

Soraya dips her ladle into the depths of a cast-iron pot. She fills blue china bowls and Jasper hands them around, serving his father first. Steam rises from each dish in deliciously fragranced curlicues. A brass teakettle sits at the edge of the embers, hissing and spitting.

"Eat, children," Soraya says as she takes her seat.

We eat with silver spoons, scooping up yellow rice, tender bits of meat (rabbit or maybe chicken, but not squirrel, surely!), sliced almonds, and plump golden raisins, seasoned with an array of mysterious spices and herbs.

With each bite, I miss Auntie more. She would be able to name every ingredient in the dish. During such a dinner, she would recount a story about the dish's origin, perhaps something about a camel herder's ugly daughter winning a nomadic prince's affections by way of her wonderful cooking. Maren has always loved such romantic tales.

After we enjoy second helpings of rice, Soraya presses an earthenware mug into my hand and gives O'Neill its twin. "Drink," she says. And so we do, moving in dance-like unison as we lift the mugs to our lips and sip the hot liquid. I taste honey, cinnamon, and black tea, and behind those pleasant flavors, a tang that hints of forbidden pleasures. My whole body warms and tingles as I drain the cup.

Jasper rises with a strange, derisive snort and stalks away.

Across from O'Neill and me, Soraya sits at her husband's feet and rests her head against his impeccably dressed knee. Dr. Phipps smiles, but not at her. He is smiling at O'Neill and me, and his smile is a wicked, wicked thing.

O'Neill wipes his mouth on his sleeve. "What was in that?" he asks. He is trembling, his shoulder shuddering against mine.

"Ah, dear boy. The devil does not share his receipts and neither do I," Dr. Phipps says. "I call it Beloved Bondage, for you shall crave it daily for the rest of your lives, needing it more than the air you breathe, and you shall be enslaved to the one who holds its secrets. That would be *me*."

The world seems to tip on its axis at this revelation, and I grab for O'Neill's arm as if he might prevent me from falling off.

O'Neill lunges toward the doctor with raised fists. "You son of a—"

"If you choose to hit me, I promise that you will be dead within the week," Dr. Phipps says calmly.

I look to Soraya for sympathy or outrage, hoping that she will object or demand that her husband grant us an antidote. Or that she will laugh and spoil his dark joke. Instead, she runs her red tongue over her lips and nestles closer to him.

Dr. Phipps takes a pocket watch from his vest and checks the hour. "It is time for you to change into your costume, Soraya my love." He leans over and kisses her noisily. And then, like a minotaur lifting a nymph, Dr. Phipps hoists his wife and clutches her to his chest. Humming, he waddles toward the tents.

"Wash those dishes quickly, Clara," Soraya calls over his shoulder. "You must not miss the show!"

O'Neill and I run to the bushes, coughing and gagging, trying to purge ourselves of the foul liquid, but it refuses to leave us.

Jasper emerges from the shadows like a ghost. "It's no use," he says. He curses and tosses a stone into the fire. "I have asked him not to use that stuff anymore, but he never listens. Why can we not be a regular traveling show with willing performers? Why must he poison each friend I make?" He kicks the dirt with his fine leather shoe and curses again.

"Help us," O'Neill begs. "Get us the antidote and we can all escape together. You could get a job in the best circus in Europe if you wanted to. I have friends who could help you."

Jasper sighs. "Alas, I am as bound to them as you are," he says. "And there is no antidote. If you do not drink daily, you die." Jasper lifts his trouser leg to his knee. His calf is tattooed with blue scrawls. "These are the names of those who have gone before you. Those who have dared to try to escape my father and his tea. Those whose bodies I have been forced to bury or burn or send down rivers."

I cover my mouth. Even in moonlight, I can count twenty names.

"Here," he says, pointing at the largest name. It is near his knee, its letters formed from flowering vines. "Zara was my wife. Papa found her performing in Canada and paid a handsome sum for her. Her own father sold her to him. She could charm the birds from the trees with her violin. She could make fireflies swarm like gnats around her body as she played and danced. Zara was the most beautiful and clever girl I'd ever met. We fell in love, but not before Papa poisoned her with his terrible tea. I didn't know what it was then, and neither did she, for he had just invented it. She drank it happily each night after dinner, and we would whisper of our plans till dawn. One afternoon while Papa and Mama were bartering with a farrier, Zara and I snuck off and found a judge to marry us. We did not tell my parents, fearing Papa's disapproval but also relishing the grand romance of a secret marriage. Eventually, we were discovered. She died soon after, and whether it was due to our son's stillbirth or Papa's wicked works, I do not know for certain."

"You are as evil as he is. You did nothing to stop us from drinking the poison," O'Neill says.

The venom in O'Neill's voice chills me. I open my mouth to speak but find I cannot. I am too disturbed for words. I am thinking of my sister, our bondage, and how badly things have turned so quickly. That what seemed like rescue led to entrapment.

"Ah," Jasper says, "what you do not know is that Papa gave me the tea on the same night he gave it to Zara. He has held my life hostage since. I do not dare oppose him. And even if I were to threaten his life, he would not tell me his secrets."

"Did you try? When you found that he had poisoned your wife, did you even try to force him to tell you?" O'Neill asks. "Or were you too cowardly to stand up to him?"

"I did try," Jasper says. "The night I lit the funeral pyre for Zara and our son. I held a knife to his throat. My hand shook so badly that I nicked him. He hides the scar beneath his cravat. He only laughed at my threats. He *dared* me to kill him. Said I'd join him in death within two days without his secret potion. So you see, there is nothing you can do but obey him, as I do."

"You have no hope of escape," I whisper. "*We* have no hope of escape."

His mouth curves in an unconvincing smile. "Well, it is not such a bad life. We travel, we sow moments of rapture, and we reap applause and money. We are adored like gods by the bored housewives and frustrated farmers we entertain." He recites these words as if reading lines from a play. "It is not such a bad life at all."

O'Neill sneers. "Except you cannot leave it for another life of your choosing."

Jasper shrugs. His face is like a mask, emotionless. Has he been enslaved so long that it seems normal to him, unremarkable? "I wish for nothing but the life I have with the show," he says.

"Wishing gets you nothing," I say.

"That is the truth," Jasper says. "Why despair over things we cannot change? And I predict that we shall have some grand adventures together on the road."

"But what of Maren?" O'Neill asks. "She will perish if she is not taken to the ocean soon."

"She may well outlive us all," Jasper says. "And she looks quite happy in that jar of hers. I half envy her simple, easy life." He wanders back to the fire and pokes it with a long stick. Sparks fly heavenward and he watches them rise and then flicker out. "Well, what is done is done, and what shall be is yet to be, and I must change into my costume. Clean up here and then go backstage. You can watch the show from there." He saunters off.

I cannot decide whether I pity Jasper or hate him.

Could he have saved O'Neill and me from bondage, or would it have cost him his life? And what would I have done in his place? His story is not my own. I do not know its complexities and what lurks in its corners, and so I cannot say. Perhaps if he had spoken out against his father tonight, Soraya would be laying the three of us out upon a funeral pyre now, right here beneath the rising crescent moon.

O'Neill limps back to a chair by the fire. He sits, head in hands, his suffering obvious. But how can I help him? I have neither balms nor elixirs to heal his body; nor do I have any words of cheer to displace his despair.

Soraya has left me a kettle of hot water, a rag, and a basin for washing the dishes. I scrub them hard, taking out my frustrations upon every bowl and spoon. Not sure what to do with them next, I pile the clean dishes on the chairs near the fire.

When I go to empty the basin in the bushes, a beady eye glints up at me.

The eye is set in a plumed black head that rests, disembodied, atop a pile of dark feathers. The sheen of these plucked feathers is familiar to me.

That poor bird was not just any bird.

I am sick to my very soul. We have eaten our dear friend Pilsner for supper.

I do not want to watch the show.

I want to take Maren's jar and steal a horse and ride to the Atlantic as fast as I can. I want O'Neill to go with me. I want Maren to be safe and well in her ocean home, and I want to go home to Llanfair Mountain and Auntie.

Wanting is as bad as wishing, I suppose, if the one who wants does nothing. Or can do nothing.

I find O'Neill backstage. He is staring into the distance. His face is pale, his forehead creased with concern.

"They served us Pilsner for supper," I blurt. I could not keep myself from telling him. I shiver as I remember finding the raven's pretty head. I sit on an overturned wooden box and try not to give way to tears. Could I ever stop weeping if I allowed myself to begin now? Could the ocean contain such a flood?

Beside me, O'Neill is perched on a wooden stool, his right leg propped on a box. When I sniffle, he hands me a handkerchief. He rests his cool hand on the back of my neck. "Pilsner was a good friend. I am sorry for your loss. For *our* loss," he says.

"It is no use being sorry," I say. "Will we do nothing about it? Will you accept his death as easily as you have accepted our Maren being put on display and ogled?" The words spill out, laced with poison like Phipps's tea. "Have you forgotten your promise to protect my sister and me? After all your time with magical gypsies, have you no idea how to escape the curse of the doctor's tea? Perhaps if you kill the owner of the curse, the curse will be broken." My whole body pulses with the pounding of my heart. Did I truly just ask O'Neill to commit murder?

He removes his hand from my neck. "How can you hold me accountable for the Phippses' treachery? It is unfair, Clara. And do you think that I have not considered every possible solution to our problems? Not for one minute have I forgotten my promises to you. But Scarff spent years teaching me to overcome my natural impulse to act rashly, and I will not risk our lives by rushing to revenge."

"Forgive me. I feel as if I am coming apart at the seams. Perhaps it is the tea's fault. Or perhaps I am changing into my true self as Maren did, only my true self is neither girl nor stork, but an ugly, mean thing. A troll or a harpy."

"You do not believe that," he says gently. "You are hurt and afraid and losing hope. Be hurt and afraid if you must, and grieve for poor Pilsner, but do not lose hope. Wouldn't Auntie give you this same advice, my dear?"

I stare at the floor. "Yes," I say, ashamed. I use O'Neill's handkerchief to dab the tears that have somehow seeped from my eyes. "But you know what they are up to, do you not? Maren is to be the main attraction in the Gallery of Wonders. They will drag her about the country and show her off until their pockets are overflowing and she dies from being kept in a jar. She is not the first mermaid they have used in such a way. Jasper wears the same tattoo as you.

And you and I will be their slaves until they tire of us—and in the end Jasper will add our names to his list."

On the other side of the red velvet curtain, the audience talks and laughs, growing louder as more voices join in. They are excited, glad for the free entertainment. Would they be so happy if they knew the utter depravity of the Phipps family?

"Look!" O'Neill says, his face turned skyward.

Osbert swoops low, his blue-scaled body almost invisible against the late afternoon sky.

"Our faithful wyvern guardian angel," O'Neill says. "Reason enough to hope a *little*, don't you think?"

Dr. Phipps climbs the steps on the opposite end of the platform and joins us backstage. "Quiet now," he says. "The show is about to begin." He walks to the place where the curtains meet and signals for them to be opened. To the side, I see Jasper pull the ropes, causing the curtains to slide apart with a whoosh.

Dr. Phipps steps forward and the crowd is instantly silent. "Ladies and gentlemen," he proclaims, "I, Dr. George Wilhelm Hieronymus Lewis Balthazar Phipps, welcome one and all to this, our astounding and spectacular entertainment! Prepare to be amazed!"

The crowd applauds. Dr. Phipps removes his hat and bows low for a count of three. Once upright again, he extends his arms and says, "I present to you the toast of the crowned heads of Europe and Asia, the beautiful chanteuse Madame Soraya of Gojanastani."

Soraya sweeps onto the stage in a sparkling gown of sunset-colored silk and a veil as sheer as candlelight. Phipps takes her hand; she curtsies low. And then he leaves her.

I did not expect the stage to be so beautiful from this vantage point. Strings of brass lanterns hang above the platform, and with the footlights they cast a golden glow upon the doctor's wife.

She begins to sing. The song is strange, its notes sliding and curving, its lyrics poignant to me even though I do not know one word of the language. Her soprano voice climbs the scale and holds a note more piercing than any I have ever heard.

"Glass would break," O'Neill says, "if she sang one note higher."

A moment later, she ends the song with a flourish of her bracelet-covered arm. Applause erupts from the audience. Soraya curtsies several times before stepping behind the curtain's edge. She comes close to us, saying, "That is how you enchant these small-town peasants. Tomorrow night, Neelo, you will perform and know the love of the crowd, the delicious devotion of strangers." Her smile, I imagine, would not look out of place on a crocodile with a belly full of fresh antelope. Her jewelry jingles as she descends from the platform and heads toward her tent.

Jasper takes the stage, carrying his violin and a wooden stool. He makes a show of flinging the tails of his expertly tailored green coat out of the way before he sits. A hush falls over the audience as he tucks the violin beneath his chin. He begins to play a slow melody, the essence of a lazy summer afternoon. He taps one foot to the beat, and the tapping grows faster as one song leads into the next. Soon, all but the feeblest spectators are on their feet, dancing and jumping and clapping.

He stands and bows; the people clamor for another song. He obliges them, choosing a tune as sweet and light as birdsong.

Dr. Phipps walks to Jasper's side, raising both arms in a grand gesture. "The great Jasper Armand shall entertain you again momentarily," he says. "First, I must deliver unto you a message of the greatest import. As a practitioner of the medical arts, I am bound by conscience to speak to you plainly, to reveal the deep secrets of healing I have gathered. Open your ears to the sound of my voice, ladies and gentlemen."

Jasper carries his instrument offstage as his father continues to speak. He winks at me as he breezes by.

Dr. Phipps's speech is almost identical to the one he gave last spring on Llanfair Mountain.

I exchange a look with O'Neill. The doctor's claim to want to heal and help all mankind does not sit well with those of us who have been drugged and deceived by him.

Half an hour later, Jasper plays a Pied Piper song on a pan flute as the townsfolk move in a mesmerized herd toward the sales tables.

"Amazing," O'Neill says.

"Disgusting," I reply. "Dr. Phipps is evil incarnate."

"Yes. Evil and charismatic. A most dangerous combination." O'Neill gets to his feet. "I have seen enough."

The music stops as Dr. Phipps returns to the stage. "Attention! Attention! I regret that I failed to invite you, one and all, to visit the large tent situated behind the stage. It is no ordinary tent, but our Gallery of Wonders! A mere five cents will gain you access to our collection of the unusual, the bizarre, and the outrageous. Wonders such as you could not imagine! Seize this opportunity by the horns, folks, or you will live with the weight of regret forever. Form a line at the door, and the famous Jasper Armand shall soon usher you in to view the secrets and curiosities of the ages!"

A pang of sorrow pierces my heart. "Maren," I whisper. "They will see her, stare at her."

"Come," O'Neill says, taking my hand. "There is nothing we can do now."

"He's right," Dr. Phipps says, startling us by poking his bewhiskered face between us. "Go to your beds, children, and do not delay. I will not have you hatching any silly plans—which would only hasten your deaths, I might add. And neither do I permit any romantic nonsense among my company. Consider yourselves forewarned on both counts. Go on, to your beds!"

As I approach my tent, I hear a rustling in a nearby tree. I look up. Two glowing eyes peer down from among the leaves. *Wyvern eyes.*

I blow a kiss to Osbert. I wish that I could invite him inside for the night. I would gladly share my pillow with him—and let him drool upon it.

I wish (for the first time in my life) that Osbert was a much bigger wyvern, one that could breathe fire on the terrible medicine show and then take to the sky while carrying Maren, O'Neill, and me on his back. Such a wyvern could carry us all the way to the ocean, and then home again to Llanfair Mountain.

But like magic, wyverns are rare in the world. Indeed, Osbert could be the last of his kind.

And what good is rescue or escape if it only ends in our dying for want of Dr. Phipps's tea?

CHAPTER TWENTY

The next morning, Dr. Phipps goes to town for a shave and haircut. Soraya retires for her midmorning nap, and Jasper slinks off dressed in fine clothes and reeking of eau de cologne—most likely to seduce some silly farm girl or faithless wife.

I finish scrubbing the pans and dishes from breakfast and then take a seat beside the dying fire. I close my eyes for a moment and imagine what Auntie might be doing now. Is she weeding her gardens or mixing up remedies for fevers? Is she delivering Hattie Benfer's yearly baby? Or is she resting on the bench by the front door, enjoying the sunshine and a cup of tea with her long-missed husband?

A poke in the ribs makes me gasp.

"O'Neill, you should not sneak up on a lady like that," I say. I smack his arm hard.

"Ladies should not be so violent," he says. "I finished mending the harnesses. Where is everyone?"

"The men have gone to town. Soraya is asleep. Osbert is watching from the white pine above the gallery tent."

He grabs my arm. "Come," he says. "We may not have another chance soon."

"Where are you taking me?"

"Do you need to ask?" Despite his limp, he pulls me along briskly, not stopping until we are inside the Gallery of Wonders.

The place is dark and smells of old wood, musty books, and lamp oil. O'Neill finds a lantern and matches on the table just inside the door.

"She should be near the back. I heard Jasper say something about a special mermaid viewing area," O'Neill says.

I follow him past tables of taxidermied animals and birds, strange things floating in jars, wooden masks and spears, artifacts enclosed in glass boxes. Finally, he pushes aside a thick gold curtain to reveal a raised platform and a glass apothecary jar containing a mermaid.

I tap on the glass. "Maren," I say. "Wake up, dear. We have come to pay you a visit."

She turns toward us with a swish. When she sees O'Neill, she bats her eyelashes and wriggles her hips so that her scales shimmer in the lantern light. She combs her fingers through her coppery hair so it floats loose about her head. She flicks her tail, flaunting her mermaidness as if O'Neill is a sailor she wishes to bring to ruin.

He turns away, his expression pained. His tattoo protects him from being utterly destroyed by her, but I know it does not save him from heartache or spare him from the normal desires of a young man.

"Maren, it is not nice to tease O'Neill like that. It's crude, and unfair to him," I scold.

She sticks out her tongue at me and then swims a few swift laps.

"It must be the liquid Soraya put her in," I say. "She is quite out of hand."

O'Neill keeps his back to Maren. "We should go," he says.

"Her locket is gone," I say. "The one you gave her for Christmas. She treasured it so."

"Stolen by Soraya, no doubt," O'Neill says. "Say your good-byes, Clara, before we are missed."

I press my hand against the glass. "Good-bye, sister," I say. "Keep well, and do try to remember your manners."

Maren stops swimming and places her hand in line with mine. From each of her sea-colored eyes falls a single pearl tear. And then she motions with her hands, asking, *When will I go to the ocean?*

She is not happy, after all.

"I do not know," I say. "We are trying to figure that out."

She motions again, telling of her love for O'Neill.

"We know that you love us, dear," I say. I will not repeat her exact sentiment to him—he has had enough torture for one day. "We love you, too. But we must go now."

O'Neill and I do not speak again until we are outside. "Thank you," I say. "I know how difficult that was for you."

"Yes. Well—"

"You are a good brother," I say. "The very best."

At the sound of approaching footsteps, he turns his head. "Phipps is coming," he says. "We must not be seen together."

I watch his back as he takes pained steps toward his tent, his shoulders slumped in a very un-O'Neill kind of way.

While O'Neill and Jasper spend the afternoon rehearsing magic tricks and juggling, I wash clothes in a nearby creek and gather greens for an early dinner—all the while thinking about the poisoned tea. (Does *it* make me think such thoughts, or are they a product of my own fears and frustrations?) From time to time,

Dr. Phipps's voice rings through the air: "Throw them higher, boy! And smile! What good is a morose juggler, I ask you?"

Perhaps if you had not poisoned us, I would like to say to him, then we might work more joyfully for you. Perhaps if you would help us deliver Maren to the sea, we would perform feats that would astound even you.

Soraya beckons me to the large wagon and commands that I remove my clothes down to the thin chemise she gave me after the fire. Horrified at the affront to my modesty, I blush from head to toe. Soraya titters like a small bird and holds forth a garment of heavy silk the color of celery, patterned with pink flowers and brown branches. "This is a kimono," she says. "In it, you will be a Japanese princess."

My arms slip into the rectangular sleeves like Maren gliding through water. Just beneath my breasts, Soraya ties long, ribbon-like strips around the kimono, stuffing the fabric one way, tugging another. As though she has dressed a hundred Japanese girls this week, she deftly wraps a wide band of pale blue around my ribs and whips its ends into a perfect bow.

"There," she says, looking pleased with her work. "Now close your eyes."

She rubs something cool and slick onto my face, and paints my lips and eyelids with a damp brush. Finally, she tells me to open my eyes. She dips a tiny brush into a little pot of black paste and outlines my eyelids. Then she uses her nimble fingers to gather my hair into a knot at the back of my head.

My curiosity gets the better of me, and I break the vow I made to myself not to speak to Soraya unless absolutely necessary. I ask, "Why are you doing this?"

"You must earn your keep. And performing is pleasure as well as work. Here is your chance to create art, to *be* art. You should thank me." She reaches into a box and pulls out a stiff-looking wig the color of Pilsner's feathers. She arranges it over my hair. It is heavy and smells of cedar and candle wax.

"Beautiful," she says, looking me over from top to toe. "Tonight, you will be part of our Gallery of Wonders. Our patrons will worship your loveliness. You will stand between the stuffed tiger cub and the African masks. I will ask Jasper to place a crate there for you, to make you a little stage of your very own."

"Am I to stand there like a statue?"

"This is your role: You play Hatsumi, a princess who has escaped her evil stepmother's house. You meet no one's eyes. You do not speak. You stare at the floor and count the sorrows of your life." Soraya smiles and tucks a stray hair under the wig. "The patrons will weep for you, poor lost flower of the Orient."

Counting my sorrows should not be a problem, I think.

But I will do this for Maren. To be near her for a few hours. To keep peace with our captors while O'Neill and I plot our escape.

Soraya smoothes the silken fabric of her sky-blue sari. "Someday, if you prove to Dr. Phipps that you can sing or dance or play an instrument, you might share the stage with Jasper and Neelo. For now, you are Hatsumi." She sets a pair of odd wooden sandals on the floor and takes my hands, helping me step into them. "You need your special tea. And then you must take your place in the gallery before our patrons begin to arrive. For them to see you outside would be unlucky, like a man seeing his bride before the wedding." She points to the door. "Hurry now, Hatsumi, to your tea. You are longing for it, are you not? Wanting it as a bee wants nectar or a leech craves blood."

When she smiles with all her teeth showing, she reminds me of a winter graveyard with two neat rows of snowy headstones.

As I wait inside the Gallery of Wonders tent, I can hear Dr. Phipps starting the show. He welcomes the townsfolk to the second night of performances, thanks them for their hospitality, praises their wisdom in purchasing his wares the previous night.

Violin music floats through the air. I imagine it is Jasper who is playing. Whoever the musician may be, the song is beautiful and haunting.

As Soraya foretold, an overturned crate awaits me between the stuffed tiger and the African masks. It is too early for me to take my place upon it. Instead, I wander down the aisles and examine the "wonders." A clamshell big enough for a cat to sleep in, a two-headed lamb floating in a jar, a costumed rat in a cage decorated like a king's quarters (he nibbles at his little throne, his lips stained red from the felted cushion), a set of a dozen mismatched eyeballs staring out of glass vials, a table of medieval torture devices, a dressmaker's form clothed in rough robes (once worn by Saint Peter, according to the sign), a bed studded with wicked-looking nails. A hundred small lanterns hang about the room, casting light and leaving shadows in all the right places.

And at the very back of the tent hangs a golden curtain, and beside the curtain hangs the sign inviting patrons to pay five cents to view "an unforgettable living spectacle, a creature of myth and magic."

My sister, the mermaid.

I step around the curtain. Inside her jar, Maren floats serenely, fast asleep. She looks no smaller than the last time I saw her, and in no worse health. But the inch-deep layer of pearls on the bottom of the jar testifies to her sadness. My salt water tears fall without a sound, and without increasing the wealth of the world.

I wipe my tears away with my fingertips, careful not to smear the thick greasepaint. I tap on the glass to awaken my sister.

With a flick of her tail and a wriggle of her belly, she comes to meet me. She looks curious and unsure until she recognizes me in my strange costume. Then she smiles and presses both hands to the glass as I do the same.

"I love you." I say, confident she can read the familiar words on my lips. And then I add, "I am so very sorry."

Maren shakes her head as if to dismiss my apology. She sinks to the bottom of the jar and curls her tail about her body. If, a year ago, she had been told that today she would be a mermaid living in a jar, enthroned on perfect pearls, she might have delighted in the romance of the notion—*if* she had not known that the pearls would be her own tears.

She motions with her hands, requesting a story.

I can hear strangers' laughter in the distance. Perhaps O'Neill is juggling spoons or frying pans; perhaps he is pulling flowers from his vest or scarves from his ears. Soon, the show will end, and after that, the strangers will pay five cents to gawk at the weird museum's exhibits, including a girl masquerading as a Japanese princess and a live mermaid imprisoned in glass.

"All right, I will tell you a short story." I lean close, hoping she can hear me. "Do you remember the year O'Neill stayed with us through the winter? He wanted to see snow. We were ten years old, yet he had never seen a single snowflake. Remember how he cried in his sleep for Scarff? Every morning his pillow had to be hung by the fire to dry. But in the daytime, what fun we had!"

Maren nods. Maybe she *can* hear through all that water and glass.

"On Christmas day, the snow came. Standing outside was like being inside one of those water globes Mr. Peterman sells, the ones you shake to make a blizzard swirl around tiny villages. That snow fell in flurries and then clumps until it piled up as high as the cottage windowsills. Auntie had to threaten us to make us go inside again, even though we could no longer feel our toes or our cherry-red cheeks. And Osbert's tail was frozen straight out like a blue icicle."

I pause, picturing Maren and O'Neill throwing snowballs at Osbert, hearing in my memory the unbridled, pure-joy laughter of my sister and my best friend.

Maren taps on the jar impatiently.

"Oh," I say. "Yes. The snowy Christmas. When Auntie forced us inside, we unwrapped ourselves from our layers of woolens and hung them to dry by the fireplace. And you were the first to notice the heavenly scent of Auntie's hot grape pudding. Steaming in our soup bowls, as purple as an Easter crocus, with dollops of whipped cream melting into froth. I can still taste it if I close my eyes. Can you?"

Maren shakes her head sadly. I do not think she remembers the taste of any food. She has not eaten in months.

"We ran our spoons around the edges of the pudding to scoop up the part that had cooled from scalding to merely hot. O'Neill giggled when he took his first bite. He said it tasted like purple heaven. He said that even without the grape pudding, it had been the best day of his life—although the day Scarff had found him under the apple tree must have been quite monumental as well. He used that word, 'monumental,' an odd word for a ten-year-old boy."

Maren is smiling again. She combs her fingers through her floating hair.

"Yet despite the joy of that day, O'Neill wept all night for Scarff. I think he wanted both worlds. But wouldn't we all have liked that—to have lived with Auntie and Scarff, together as a family? But we know now that it was the curse that kept us apart."

In my mind's eye, I can see him, the boy O'Neill. Almost always grinning, almost always up to some sort of gentle mischief (for which he would receive instant forgiveness from all—except the grudge-holding cat). My memories show me the unruly crop of blond hair that sprouted from his head like stalks of grain sown in crooked rows, the gap between his front teeth, and the way he'd usually forget to button half the buttons on his shirt. A bit of a wild thing he was, a creature raised by an absentminded traveling merchant. The hours Auntie spent trying to teach him manners! The hours he wriggled and played dumb just to tease her!

But we loved that boy, and he loved us.

He loves us still. And he loves Maren most of all.

"Maren, what if this had not happened," I say slowly, "and you had not become a mermaid? What if O'Neill—"

"Clara!" Jasper calls from the doorway. "Are you bothering the mermaid again? You should be on your box, preparing to bask in the adoration of our guests."

I slip out from behind the curtain. "She is my sister. I do not *bother* her."

Dressed in a ridiculous pirate costume, Jasper strides toward me, hands on hips. "Stare if you must. I know that I am handsome," he says. "Practically irresistible, truth be told."

I ignore his comments and step onto my box, careful not to snag the sumptuous fabric of the kimono. "There. I am in place. No harm done."

"I must say that you look almost as irresistible as I do," Jasper says. He fingers my sash. "It suits you, you know. You should always wear silk, day and night."

"Jasper!" Soraya scolds from just outside. "Take your place to collect the money, son. The customers are coming."

He struts away as if he truly believes himself a dashing seafarer.

"Stand up straight, Clara child," Soraya commands from the doorway. "You are a princess, not a farm girl. Keep your eyes to the floor, and do not speak, no matter what anyone says to you."

The patrons begin to file in, brushing past Soraya. They *ooh* and *ahh* as they peruse the oddities laid out before them on tables and shelves.

As instructed, I gaze steadily at my hem.

I think about the snowy Christmas, and the three snow angels we pressed into the whiteness beside the red barn. As we raised and lowered our arms to create wings, the tips of our mittens brushed together and we were one instead of three. Not orphans or foundlings, not friends or siblings, but one entity. Cold and wet and happy beyond description.

A tug on my sleeve shocks me out of my daydream.

"Pretty little thing, ain't you?" a gravelly voice says, too close to my painted face. "I heard what your kind is good for, and I'll pay you more than five cents for it, sweetheart." His breath reeks of sour tobacco and moldy cheese. His hand moves in a circle on my shoulder, then begins to slip lower.

I bring my knee up swiftly. Amid his agonized yowling, I resume my statue-like pose, eyes downcast, smile faint and demure. He ought not to have insulted this princess.

Dr. Phipps appears out of nowhere and, grabbing the lout by his coat collar, drags him toward the door.

"Dear me, folks," Phipps declares dramatically, "this poor gentleman seems to be having an attack of the bilious fever! But do not panic, for I have the cure for that very ailment. Yes, sir. Right this way. I will have you fit as a fiddle in the blink of Zeus's great eye!"

Then and there, I resolve to learn to juggle live rats if that is what it takes to be removed from the role of Princess Hatsumi.

"Line up here, if you please," I hear Soraya say. She is at the back of the tent now. "Single file. You will each be granted a one-minute visitation with the beautiful divinity awaiting you behind this curtain. You will never forget her, even if you live for a thousand years. Come, come! For just five cents, you may behold the splendor of our live mermaid!"

A hush falls over the room but lifts quickly. Many voices speak at once.

"Did she say *mermaid*?"

"It's a trick. All paste and horsehide."

"My uncle saw a mermaid when he served in the British Navy."

"Can I have the money, Mama? I want to see it. Please?"

"If it's alive, I'll eat my hat, Mabel!"

I tilt my head slightly so I can watch that end of the tent from the corner of my eye. The first person in line is a teenaged boy. He drops his pennies into Soraya's coin box and steps behind the curtain.

"Please do not tap upon the glass or bother the mermaid with loud noises. She is a sensitive creature," Soraya says.

From behind the curtain, the teenager says, "Oh, glory!"

"Move along, sir," Soraya says. "Next please."

The boy emerges, rubbing his forehead and smiling like a drunken clown.

Time and time again, the male customers come out from behind the curtain with similar expressions, somewhere between lovesick and stupefied. The females look jealous or skeptical. All the children have shiny Christmas-morning faces.

Guilt washes over me. I should have been able to protect my sister from being put on display for profit. From being ogled like the two-headed lamb or the collection of eyeballs. I want to hop off my crate and rescue her, but I feel Dr. Phipps's gaze upon me, and I know that to attempt to take Maren now would buy my death and leave her at his mercy however long she might live.

An hour later, or maybe two, the last gawker exits the tent. Every bone and muscle in my body aches from remaining still for so long. My feet throb, and I wonder if real Japanese princesses are forced to wear such uncomfortable shoes.

"It is time for bed," Soraya says. Her money box rattles as she saunters past me. "You will need your rest. In the morning, we pack and take to the road again. This is hard work, is it not? The life of the entertainer."

Wearily, I nod.

"One thing before I go," she says coolly. "You will not assault a paying customer again. If you feel you are being threatened, cough loudly and I will come to your aid. Your behavior this evening was most undignified, and could have meant a loss of profit for Dr. Phipps. And you know it is our duty to keep Dr. Phipps happy."

I nod again with the poise of Princess Hatsumi. Inside, my anger simmers.

"I am glad we understand one another," she says. "Now, douse all the lamps in the gallery, and then go straight to bed."

I do not go to the wagon to sleep. Instead, I go to Maren. On her bed of pearls, she slumbers as peacefully as a baby.

"Good night, sister," I say. I kick off the horrid wooden sandals and wrap myself in the blue velvet formerly used to cover her jar. I lie down beside her on the dirt floor.

I sleep, and I dream of growing white feathered wings and a long red bill. I dream of pulling Maren from her jar with my clawed toes and lifting her above the tent. My wings catch the wind and I carry my sister through cloudless skies all the way to the sea.

CHAPTER TWENTY-ONE

In the next town, I beg to be taught a show-worthy skill. O'Neill spends two hours schooling me in the art of juggling. He is a patient teacher indeed. When he stands close to me, the warmth radiating from his skin makes me weak in the knees. He cups my hands in his, forcing me to toss the balls high into the air. He whispers instructions and encouragements into my ear. I could melt into the earth.

Silently, I scold my wayward heart and remind it that O'Neill loves my sister, and she loves him.

As I fumble with the colored balls, O'Neill groans and rolls his eyes. Jasper howls dementedly, seeming to find it especially hilarious when the balls bounce off my head and shoulders.

I am not so amused. I do not relish the thought of spending another evening as Princess Hatsumi. Still, if that is my fate, at least I will be in the same room as Maren.

Jasper sits down on a tree stump and sighs. "You will never be a juggler, Clara. Unless . . ." A wicked grin blossoms between his nose and chin, "Unless you become Clumsy Clara the Clown. I believe we have a clown costume somewhere."

O'Neill laughs as if he and Jasper are great friends. He should not behave so.

"Well, that is out of the question," I declare. "I dislike clowns, and I will not be one."

"Hmm," O'Neill says, regaining his composure. "What about a magician's assistant? I've been studying a book I found in the wagon and I recall reading of several illusions we could perform together."

"Will I be sawed in two? I would really rather stay in one piece," I say.

"No sawing, I promise," O'Neill says. "But I could make you vanish. Or you could hand me props for other tricks."

"Smashing idea," Jasper says. "And Mama has just the gown for you, all spangled and barely decent."

I think he is serious. I refuse to further his amusement by expressing my horror at the thought of the immodest dress.

Jasper jumps to his feet. "I'll just hurry over and ask Papa doctor and Mama what they think of the idea. Then I'll find that fabulous gown for you to try." He winks at me roguishly before walking away.

"There," says O'Neill. "Problem solved."

"One of them," I say. "And not the most pressing one. We are no closer today to finding a way to deliver Maren to the ocean than we were the day Phipps first dosed us. Time is passing, and her chances with it."

"Not so loud, Clara," O'Neill says. "First of all, do as I do, and feign friendship. Or at least submission. You must not cause the slightest suspicion." He leans closer, resting his cheek against mine as he whispers in my ear. "I have been thinking about Maren's dilemma, every minute of every day. I will find a way to take her to the ocean, Clara. If I have to die to do it, I will."

"What's all this?" Dr. Phipps's voice bellows behind us. "Lovers' murmurings, perhaps?"

"Perhaps," O'Neill says without missing a beat.

"Well, fair Romeo, you are needed for some honest work. Madame Phipps wishes to rearrange the artifacts in the Gallery of Wonders and requires brute strength. Get thee hence before she becomes a gorgon and transforms us all to stone."

I do not care for his attempts at humor. I know he is a devil, and nothing he can say will make me smile.

O'Neill tips an imaginary hat and leaves us. I watch him go, glad to see that he is hardly limping today. Dr. Phipps grips my arm with one leather-gloved hand and grabs my jaw with the other. His touch is neither gentle nor kind.

"Be careful, little Clara," he says. He calls me little, but he is only a few inches taller than I, and his shoes are made with extra-thick soles to elevate him. His breath smells of stale coffee and sardines. "Your face betrays your rebellious thoughts. You think you are so very clever. But you must remember to whom you belong now. You must remember whose power holds sway over your very life. You should remember and be in awe."

I shudder. Not from fear, but from revulsion.

"You are trembling, little one." Dr. Phipps laughs grimly and drops his hands to his sides. "Now you have given me my due. Be a good girl and get the fire going. And no more silly lovers' meetings. Affairs between servants never end well, especially when the servants are addicted to my Beloved Bondage tea. Ask Jasper if you do not believe me."

I stare at my shoes until the sound of Dr. Phipps's footsteps fades away.

Such an evil, evil man is Dr. Phipps. I almost wish Osbert would eat him.

CHAPTER TWENTY-TWO

I am gathering firewood in a grove of birch and hemlock trees. It is just after dawn, and I must feed the embers of last night's campfire so that Dr. Phipps may have his morning porridge on time. The man lives by his pocket watch—a strange practice for a nomadic fellow. Scarff, the true wayfarer, has always hated clocks and watches. O'Neill told me that Scarff once threw a gold pocket watch into the gaping mouth of an alligator because the incessant ticking drove him to distraction. I suspect there is more to that tale, as Scarff is not the sort to toss valuables aside so easily.

Something stirs in the branches above my head. Something much bigger than a squirrel. I look up just as the thing swoops down and knocks me to the ground.

A rough tongue bathes my face. "Osbert!" I cry, hugging the scaly beast.

The wyvern sits back on his tail and grins. He lifts one foot to show me the suede pouch between his talons.

"Is that for me?" I ask.

He nods and opens his mouth. The pouch falls into my hands and I quickly pry open the cinched top. Inside I find a small leather scabbard, and within the scabbard is a dagger. The dagger is plain—without jeweled hilt or engraving—but the blade fairly sings with sharpness.

"Osbert, what am I to do with this?"

He wags his barbed tail and cocks his head to one side.

"Well, thank you," I say, patting him between the pointy ears. "Good boy."

"Clara!" Jasper's voice echoes through the trees. "Where are you?"

Osbert flaps his wings and returns to the camouflage of the treetops. I sheathe the blade and hide it in the deep pockets of the skirt Soraya gave me to wear for servant work.

"I'm here," I say. "Collecting firewood."

"Hurry back," Jasper shouts. "Papa wants an early breakfast. He has decided to move on today instead of tomorrow."

"Grand," I mutter. "It seems that even the reliable cannot be relied upon."

I pick up the sticks I dropped in the wyvern attack. "Osbert," I whisper to the treetops. "Follow closely, but not too closely. I will meet you again as soon as it is safe for us both. I'll use the mourning dove cry, in three groups of three. Wiggle a branch if you understand."

Far above, a hemlock bough sways, raining tiny fir cones upon my head.

"Clara!" Jasper shouts impatiently.

"Coming!" I reply just as testily. But for all my irritation at being disturbed by Jasper, my heart is glad. I have been with dear Osbert, and he has armed me well—even though I do not intend to stab anyone anytime soon.

O'Neill is brushing one of the horses as I pass by with my armload of wood. Without slowing my gait, I whisper, "Osbert paid me a call."

"Good morning," O'Neill says, emphasizing the "good."

"Hurry, child!" Soraya calls from beside the smoldering embers. "Dr. Phipps is a bear this morning. We must soothe him with his breakfast. Drop the sticks there and fetch the sack of dried berries from the hutch in the wagon. Second drawer." Her forehead is creased with worry.

Jasper follows me into the wagon. "Stay clear of Papa today," he warns. "The last time he was in such a foul mood, I was forced to dig a grave. Our clumsy young servant girl Florry—or was it Nadine? Well, no matter. She tripped and splashed him with hot coffee, and that was the end of her. It was a shame. She was the most talented harpist, and she had the body of a goddess."

"What did he do to her?" I ask, but quickly change my mind about wanting to know. "No, please don't tell me." I locate the small sack of berries and turn to go.

"Listen," he says. "I like you and O'Neill. More than I should. You must be careful."

"I will," I say, surprised at his great concern.

He reaches out and cups my shoulders with his hands. "Papa swears that last night he saw in the flesh the thing of his nightmares, the thing that a fortune-teller once said would bring his death. He is frantic with fear. And when Papa is fearful, his temper is short. We are all in danger at such times. Even Soraya bears scars to testify to that."

"I promise to be wary," I say. "Thank you for your advice."

Soraya calls me again, and I brush past Jasper and hurry to do her bidding.

I wonder about Dr. Phipps's nightmare monster. Strange how its sighting coincides with Osbert's visit. Could Osbert be the instrument of his doom? I cannot imagine Osbert killing a person. The largest thing he has ever killed was a fox he found digging its way into the chicken coop. But a wyvern is a dragon, and dragons do have a history of man-killing.

I wish to escape, certainly, but there must be a less violent way to go about it. One that does not involve my pet wyvern acquiring a taste for human blood.

The dagger bumps against my hip as I walk. I wonder if *it* has tasted human blood, and if it might do so again.

What would I do to save my sister? What might I do to save O'Neill? I would give my life. But would I give someone else's? Could I?

I hope that it will never come to that.

I wish I could be certain.

Jasper was right.

Today, his father is a black cloud full of explosive thunder and dangerous lightning. He leaves in his wake broken dishes, nervous horses, and a wife drenched in tears.

Dr. Phipps paces and mutters like a madman. He commands Jasper to bring the mermaid into the large wagon. Jasper is to watch over their priceless main attraction as Dr. Phipps drives. Jasper must also keep an eye on O'Neill and me, in case we are plotting mutiny or elopement. Soraya must drive the smaller wagon alone. When she hears this, her wailing grows more and more intense until Phipps threatens to beat her if she does not cease *at once*.

When the packing is done, and Soraya is installed upon her driver's seat, Dr. Phipps whips the horses into a gallop that almost lifts the wagon wheels from the ground.

Every dish, treasure, and artifact rattles as we rush along. The water in Maren's jar sloshes to and fro; her small body bumps into the glass over and over. If mermaids bruise, she will be black-and-blue by nightfall. No one speaks. No one dares to mention that Dr. Phipps is killing the horses by running them so mercilessly for so long.

Pearls the size of poppy seeds fall from Maren's eyes and drift about her like snow. O'Neill and I exchange concerned glances. But there is nothing we can do to end her discomfort.

Jasper stares at Maren, his expression detached—as though he is observing a tadpole instead of a thinking, feeling, and cherished *person*.

I decide to test him to see if he will tell the truth about his protective tattoo: "How are you able to gaze at Maren that way without consequence, while the men who pay to look at her for a single minute become blathering fools?"

"Mermaids are not so fascinating once you've known a few. And perhaps I've built up a resistance. Anyway, I find girls with legs much more appealing than girls with fins," Jasper says, leering at me. "That pink bodice suits you, Clara. The color makes your skin look like fresh cream."

My face heats. "You are not behaving like a gentleman," I say. I look to O'Neill and see anger in his eyes. I shake my head, silently warning him not to get into trouble with Jasper on my account.

"You never want to play, Clara. I find it quite disheartening." Jasper leans back into a pile of fat cushions. "I might as well nap. Just remember, I'm only a few feet away if you get lonely."

"Jasper, please show some respect," O'Neill says in a polite but strained tone.

"You both bore me terribly." Jasper closes his eyes. Soon, his head lolls and he sleeps—in spite of being jostled about in the careening wagon.

I reach deep into my skirt pocket. O'Neill raises his eyebrows.

I move to his side and am almost thrown into his lap as the wagon whips around a corner. He takes my arm to steady me.

"Thank you," I whisper, kneeling beside him. "Look. Osbert brought this." I place the scabbard in his hand.

Carefully, he slides the dagger from its sheath. "That is dangerous looking indeed."

"My thought exactly. You should keep it," I say.

"No. It is yours. Osbert chose to give it to you. He must have had his reasons for doing so."

"But I could never use such a thing," I say. "Except to open letters or slice cheese."

"Save it for cheese, then. It is yours." He returns the weapon to me. "But perhaps you will need it for something else. To save me from a sea monster. To defend my honor among unruly wenches."

"Very amusing," I say. I put the scabbard back into my pocket.

"I would not be surprised if it is endued with strong magic of some kind. Sometimes the plainest of things conceal the most unimaginable wonders," he says. He peers at me oddly, as if searching for something behind my eyes. Then he sighs and lays his head upon my shoulder. "This is not the way I thought this story would be told."

"Story?" I rest my head on his. The speeding carriage hits a bump and knocks our skulls together painfully. We both sit up straight and check for blood.

He rubs the sore spot above his ear. "You know, the story of our lives. I meant to be the great hero. I meant to save Maren and to make both of you blissfully happy."

"O'Neill," I say. "You have always made Maren and me happy."

Jasper snores in piglike snorts. O'Neill continues. "I had a plan: a big house for all of us, with a solarium for Auntie's herbs, a huge workshop for Scarff, a fine parlor for Maren to take tea in, and a library for you. Rooms for a dozen children. Even a ballroom for dancing. We would have had the most magnificent Christmas parties. But I suppose none of it is possible now."

"This story is not yet finished," I remind him. With all my being, I want to reach out to comfort him. Instead, I keep my hands folded in my lap. "You have told me again and again to hold on to hope. You must do the same." I will not remind him that Maren is a mermaid now, and will never again be a tea-drinking young lady.

O'Neill reaches inside his jacket sleeve and pulls out a daisy, its slim white petals perfect and uncrushed. "For you," he says.

I accept his gift and try not to blush. "Thank you."

"What ending would you wish for, Clara?" he asks.

"Have you forgotten the message carved into the tree beside the Wishing Pool? 'Wishing gets you nothing.'"

"Who is the pessimist now?" He nudges me with his elbow. "That sign is ridiculous," he says. "It should be destroyed."

"I dare you to do it!" A smile invades my face and heart.

"All right, I will." He raises his right hand and speaks solemnly, "I swear by the stars and the moon and Auntie's plum cake that I, O'Neill of the Apple Tree, shall destroy the fallacious sign that maligns the Wishing Pool on Llanfair Mountain. I shall burn it and throw its foul ashes into the cesspit!"

We both laugh. It is a good moment, one I plan to treasure, whatever our ending may be.

Suddenly, the wagon lurches, and the terrible cry of an injured horse rends the air. The wagon jerks to a halt, sending boxes and baskets flying and tipping Maren's jar to its side.

O'Neill and I struggle to our feet and hurry to right the jar. The pearls slosh to the bottom. Maren signs that she is not hurt.

Jasper wakes up swearing and pushes a box off his legs. "Now what? You wait here, and I'll find out why we've stopped."

"It's Hippocrates, the bay horse. His leg is broken," O'Neill says after Jasper leaves. "There is no mistaking the meaning of that cry."

Furious shouts almost overpower the horse's wails of pain. Dr. Phipps calls down curses upon all horses, upon all fortune-tellers, upon all ill-repaired roads, upon the entire earth and all of humanity.

The volume and vehemence of the doctor's curses unsettle me. I look to O'Neill for reassurance, and he takes my hand.

The shouting stops. I hear a gunshot, and the horse's cries cease. But the silence lasts only seconds before Soraya begins to wail.

"Stay here," O'Neill says. He steps over fallen boxes and baskets until he reaches the little sliding window that opens to the driver's seat. He peers out.

"What has happened?" I ask.

"Hippocrates is dead. Jasper and Soraya are kneeling on the ground beside Phipps," O'Neill says.

"Dr. Phipps is dead, too? Then the prophecy of the monster did not come true."

"He may still live. I cannot tell from here. I'm going out. Will you come?" O'Neill hurries toward the door, picking a path through more debris.

I glance at Maren, who is sleeping peacefully now that the wagon's wild motions have ceased. I follow O'Neill.

"Poor Hippocrates," O'Neill says as we come upon the bloody scene. "He was a gentle soul."

"There you are, O'Neill," Jasper says, scrambling to his feet. "Give us a hand getting Papa into the wagon. He's had some sort of fit. He's unconscious."

"Please, boys," Soraya says, "be careful with him. He is not well, not at all well." She sobs into her veil. How she can love such a wicked brute, I will never understand. Perhaps he slipped an exceptionally powerful love potion into her tea many years ago.

I go ahead of them and arrange the cushions on Soraya's couch, making room for the doctor's limp body.

Once Jasper and O'Neill install him there, Soraya covers him with a blanket and lifts his hand to her moist cheek. "Please wake up, my love," she says.

"Rest is what he needs, Mama," Jasper says. "He has overtaxed himself."

"Yes, my son," Soraya says, "that is true. He needs rest." She loosens her husband's cravat and unbuttons his vest and shirt. She fusses with his hair and adjusts the blanket.

"We must move the wagons off the road," Jasper says. "We'll have to make camp until we find another horse."

"Yes, son," Soraya says. "You take care of these things. I will take care of your poor father. Oh, my darling George! My love!" She covers his face with kisses.

Whatever love potion she imbibed was very strong indeed.

CHAPTER TWENTY-THREE

The sun wears a fiery orange halo as I watch it sinking beyond the rolling acres of cornfields. Crickets sing and a few fireflies rise up from the grass, flashing their secret signals to one another. Tonight's dinner bubbles in the pot: a rabbit stew flavored with wild herbs and a few spices from Soraya's well-stocked cabinet.

Jasper and O'Neill approach the fireside almost soundlessly. They set Maren's jar beside me, presenting her as though she is a gift. Which, of course, she is. My sister swims in circles and waves her tiny hand at me. She presses her palms to the glass and stares at the campfire's bright flames. My sister has always loved a campfire—perhaps because it is not something someone born of water ought to do.

With Dr. Phipps laid up in the wagon and Soraya scrutinizing his every twitch, O'Neill, Jasper, Maren, and I have gained a measure of freedom.

"This is Scarff's kind of night," O'Neill says as he sits cross-legged between Maren and me. "A nice half-moon rising, peeper frogs peeping, the air perfumed with stew and wood smoke, and a pretty lass or two to admire."

"Pretty lasses!" I say. "I thought Scarff was devoted to Auntie, his *wife*!"

"Well, he only *looked*," O'Neill says wryly. "Truly, Clara, he liked the lasses around for their cooking. The fellow burned everything he ever put in a pan, even water! But in all our days together, Scarff never spoke of anyone as fondly as he did of Auntie Verity. And her two girls."

Jasper sits opposite me and begins cleaning his fingernails with a pocketknife. "Is he flirting with you again, Clara? Does he never stop?"

"Don't be silly, Jasper. He's practically my brother." I wish I could crawl under a very large rock.

"*Practically* does not a brother make," Jasper says. "But if that is what you believe, Clara . . ."

Maren frowns, her eyes glinting at Jasper. O'Neill is hers, she would tell Jasper if she could speak. She flicks her tail menacingly, and waves form atop the water. I think it would be unwise to tangle with an angry mermaid, even one as small as she.

Jasper shrugs. "So be it, then. What I would like to know is this: Is my dinner ready yet, woman?" He uncaps a silver flask and drinks.

I throw a handful of grass at Jasper. "Get it yourself," I say, smiling as if in jest—although I mean what I say. "I may be your father's slave, but I am not yours."

"Ouch," Jasper says. "I am undone by your bitter words, my lady."

"Good. You needed some undoing," I say, playing along. Things are changing since the doctor's fit, and making Jasper believe I am his friend may soon prove advantageous. "And while you're getting your stew, would you mind getting mine?"

"Ah, Jasper! Never vex one of Verity's girls," O'Neill says. "You'll pay the price, and then be forced to pay it again!"

"Both of you should fill your mouths with food instead of words for a change," I say, and I get up to do the serving.

After I am seated again, I turn my attention to my sister for a moment. Now reclining upon the pearls in the bottom of her jar, Maren has regained her peaceful demeanor. She combs her fingers through her coppery hair and then begins braiding a section of it.

"How is your father?" I ask Jasper between bites.

"The same," Jasper says, sounding unconcerned. "But rest assured. Once I purchase a new horse, we will be on our way again. As they say, 'The show must go on.'" He holds out his bowl, demanding more without asking. "I thought we could try a few new acts while Papa doctor is under the weather. O'Neill tells me he can eat fire, and I am positively dying to see you onstage in one of Mama's flimsy dancing costumes, Clara."

I fill his bowl, wishing I could dump its contents over his unmannerly head.

"Clara was brought up to be modest, Jasper," O'Neill says. "Is that not something to be valued in a young lady?"

"A young *nun*, perhaps. Clara has no idea how to enjoy life. I am only offering to help her open up to the possibilities of experience and sensation. You could use some unbuttoning yourself, O'Neill." Jasper stands and reaches inside his jacket. He takes out his pennywhistle. "Let me help you. I will play you a tune, and you will dance. You will have fun tonight, even if I must make you."

I glance at Maren. She sleeps, completely undisturbed by Jasper's advances. For once, I am jealous of her.

Jasper plays a merry jig. O'Neill stands, takes my hand, and pulls me to my feet. "Keep playing along, Clara," he whispers. "For Maren's sake." He twirls me about.

And so I imagine we are dancing next to one of Auntie's bonfires, surrounded by frolicking Llanfair Mountain children. I picture Scarff playing the songs, and Maren dancing with one of the Fischer boys. I focus on O'Neill's familiar face and pretend that we have not a care in the world. For a few minutes, I dare to let joy bubble up inside me.

After several songs, Jasper asks O'Neill, "Do you play?"

"I do," he says, bent over with hands on thighs, trying to catch his breath. His limp has all but disappeared but he is still not as strong as he was before the caravan fire.

Jasper hands him the pennywhistle. "Something slow and sweet," he says. He bows to me, saying, "May I have this dance?"

"I am tired," I say. "I would like to rest."

"Nonsense. I just used my best manners, and therefore you must dance with me. Just one song, I promise." Jasper takes my hand and places his arm about my waist. "Don't be scared. I am not an ogre."

O'Neill plays a beautiful tune, and Jasper waltzes me around the fire. When we reach the far side of it, he whispers, "Why do you despise me so, Clara?" His speech is slurred, his breath whiskey-scented.

I turn my head and lean back. I can think of no safe way to answer his question.

He smiles like a hungry fairy-tale wolf. "You are not at all my type. You're far too sweet and plain. Nothing like my Zara. Yet I am fascinated by you. I dream of you, you know. I dream of us together, traveling the world, performing for royalty. I dream of covering you with jewels and fine dresses, spoiling you with delights."

"Please do not say such things," I say. I try to pull away, but his grip tightens.

"Clara," he whispers, his hot breath on my earlobe, "you have bewitched me."

The song ends abruptly. "It is late," O'Neill says, "and we should sleep."

Jasper releases me. His eyes are glassy with the exact look that boys have after seeing the mermaid. It sends a shiver up my spine.

"We shall camp beneath the stars," Jasper proclaims. "Fetch the blankets, Clara."

Inside my pocket, the dagger bumps against my leg as I walk to the wagon. If Jasper does not mind his manners, he may become acquainted with the fearsome weapon.

Hours later, Jasper and O'Neill sleep cocooned in blankets on the opposite side of the fire. I lie beside Maren's jar and watch the moon inch its way across the spangled cloth of the heavens. I despair of ever falling asleep.

Suddenly, I realize: none of us have drunk our compulsory cup of Beloved Bondage tea tonight.

And I do not crave it at all—nor do I feel the least bit sickly.

Someone has been lying to us.

Dawn's pink light dyes the clouds above our camp. I stand beside O'Neill's blanket-wrapped, prostrate body and nudge him awake with my foot.

"Five more minutes," he says, moaning.

I kneel beside him. "Hush," I whisper. "Don't wake Jasper. You must come with me to gather firewood. *Now*, O'Neill."

Without further complaint, he untangles himself from his blankets and follows me into a copse of old trees.

Once the camp is out of sight, I stop and lean against a thick oak. "How do you feel?" I ask.

He runs a hand through his thatch of hair. "You want to know how I feel? About what, precisely?"

"Good heavens, O'Neill," I say a bit too loudly. "I mean *physically*. Do you feel sick, or dizzy, or weak?"

"Oh." He yawns. "Despite being rudely awakened, I feel fine. Actually, I feel quite well. And you?"

"Fine. But I am not trying to make polite conversation. I am asking because we did not drink Dr. Phipps's tea last night. We should be ill by now, stricken with desperate craving, as he said would happen if we missed a dose. But here we stand, unaffected."

"He lied," O'Neill says. "The dirty old fiend."

"I think Jasper lied, too. I think he made up that story about the name tattoos and his wife."

"Perhaps," he says. "But it would not be prudent to ask him. Jasper does his best to portray the doctor as wicked and dangerous, but he is ten times worse. He is obsessed with making the Phipps show world renowned, and he believes the mermaid is the key. Every day he warns me, without saying so directly, that he will kill me if I try to take Maren. He thinks you are putting me up to it. That I am under your spell or something."

"He says those things?"

"When we are alone in our tent, he tells stories. Allegories of a gullible young man in love with an enchantress who persuades him to steal the king's most treasured possession. The king inevitably catches them and sentences them to violent deaths. Evisceration, twin guillotines, drawing and quartering. Dreadful stuff."

"He is mad," I say.

"I am afraid so." O'Neill's dear face looks so very grim.

"All the more reason to plan our escape. You must think, O'Neill. Think hard, and I will as well. There must be some way."

"I've thought of little else since the fire," he says. "Meanwhile, we must prepare. We need to find a smaller vessel for transporting Maren. Something that can be moved without the brute strength of two grown men."

Behind us, twigs crack and snap beneath someone's feet.

"Kiss me," O'Neill says.

"What?"

Before I can object, he pulls me into his arms and presses his mouth to mine. I feel like I am melting, like I am a blazing candle melting into a pool of liquid wax. Time and the universe seem to disappear. There is nothing in the world but O'Neill.

"Ha!" Jasper's voice interrupts my elation. "I knew it! I knew you two were hiding something. 'He's like my brother!' says Clara. Ha!" He grins, but his tone is bitter. "I should have guessed there was a reason you resisted me last night, you little minx. I should have known your virginal rebukes were nothing but an act."

I step out of O'Neill's embrace, my knees trembling and my heart racing.

"Well, you've caught us," O'Neill says boldly. He takes my hand and holds it to his chest. "Clara, darling, it was a delicious secret. But no more."

His acting is superb. His eyes sparkle as he hides a kiss in my palm.

"Enough!" Jasper says. "Go back to keeping it secret, would you? Anyway, I did not come here looking to find a lovers' tryst. I came to find you, O'Neill, so that we could venture into town and buy a horse. Because, as you so often boast, you know horses like you know your own left foot. Whatever that may mean."

"Right," O'Neill says, releasing my hand. "I will help you gather wood later, Clara."

Jasper slaps O'Neill on the back, a little too hard for a friendly gesture. "Is that your code now? Perhaps Clara would like to 'gather wood' with *me* later." He pushes O'Neill along the path. What was O'Neill thinking, provoking a madman to jealousy?

Well, it cannot be undone.

And would I wish for it to be undone?

As I pick up twigs, as I step over fallen branches, as I bundle kindling and tie it with lengths of young wild grape vine, I think of the kiss. My first kiss. How I would give a year of my life to have it back, just so I could have it once more from him.

But O'Neill loves Maren, doesn't he?

Or has that changed somehow? Could I dare to hope for such a thing? Would it be wrong to hope for it?

I am so confused. My stomach churns. Maybe I *did* need that dose of tea, after all. Maybe O'Neill did, too. Maybe we are both insane from the lack of it.

My foot catches in a tree root and I fall facedown into a patch of moss. O'Neill pulls me to my feet and wipes away the bits of green fluff clinging to my cheek and hair. I cannot decide what the look in his eyes means, why he has come back.

"Sorry," he whispers as he hands me the kindling.

"For what?"

"You know. The kiss."

"Oh," I say. I look at the ground as Princess Hatsumi would and I try to gather enough pride to keep from bursting into tears.

"I didn't know what else to do when I heard him coming. I panicked."

"It is fine," I say as my heart shatters. "You did what had to be done."

"Come on, O'Neill," Jasper shouts. "Where are you now? Not kissing again, I hope! Let's get on the road, shall we?"

I follow O'Neill out of the woods. My eyes are dry, but inside I am weeping.

Yet would I wish he had never kissed me? Honestly, I cannot say.

As I stir the porridge, I hate O'Neill.

As I spoon the porridge into Dr. Phipps's favorite blue-and-white china bowl, I love O'Neill more than life itself.

As I fetch water from the creek for Soraya (so that she might bathe her husband's pale face), I detest O'Neill.

As I sit beside Maren and mend a skirt Soraya gave me (stabbing the needle through the fabric and yanking the thread into an ugly row of puckered stitches), I hate him with a passion. He had no right to give that kiss to me—it ought to have been Maren's.

I hate him for stealing my first kiss from me. It was precious, and he robbed me of it.

Was it *his* first kiss? Or did some gypsy girl claim that from him long ago, under a full moon, beside a lake full of alligators and flying fish?

I touch my mouth, remembering the pressure of his lips, the warmth of his breath, how he tasted of summer rainstorms. I love him, and it is wrong. And hopeless.

Maren taps on the glass. She questions me with her eyes. As she has since we were infants, she senses when I am troubled. "It's nothing," I lie. "The sun is so bright today that it is giving me a headache."

She shakes her head, clearly unconvinced by my falsehood.

"Did I show you this skirt?" I hold it high, hoping she might focus upon it instead of my face. My lower lip quivers. "Look at the embroidery along the edge. Can you see the little deer and trees? It must have taken a year to sew such an intricate pattern." I am choking on tears.

Soraya beckons me, and I am relieved. "I will be back soon, sister," I say. I set my sewing beside the mermaid's jar and flee her searching gaze.

I hate O'Neill.

Almost as much as I hate myself.

Chapter Twenty-Four

The contents of Soraya's cauldron boil and bubble over into the fire with a loud hissing, all but obscuring the birds' twilight songs. A heady aroma spews forth and swirls through the air: the stench of simmering bones, garlic, sassafras bark, peculiar pink-and-yellow powders, and one of Dr. Phipps's woolen socks. I hold a handkerchief over my face in a futile attempt to avoid breathing the tainted air.

I remember countless hours spent stirring Auntie's mixtures over an outdoor fire. Some of them are pungent, to be sure—but none reek as much as Soraya's. Auntie cooks up potions to cure warts, elixirs to clear congested lungs, syrups to tame aching stomachs . . . as many as a hundred different medicines in a season. The day before I took to the road with Maren and O'Neill, I helped Auntie make a potent sleeping draught. I am surprised by how much I miss such a mundane task.

A sleeping draught, I think.

Such a simple thing might be our salvation.

It is a thought to mull over.

"Do you really believe that will help Papa?" Jasper says, pinching his nostrils. "It smells like a possum carcass rolled in fish guts."

Soraya stirs the sputtering concoction with a long-handled wooden spoon. "Of course. It is an ancient remedy my mother taught me. If it smelled good, it would not be so powerful."

Inside her jar, Maren is blessedly unbothered by the smell. I watch her for a moment, floating like a small angel in a cloudless sky. Not that I have ever heard of an angel with a fish's tail.

Poor Maren. She is shrinking again, bit by bit, and she is increasingly listless. While Soraya has been caring for her husband, she has neglected to add the mysterious preservatives to our mermaid's jar.

O'Neill, too, is watching Maren. The expression on his face cannot be named. There is no word for the emotion between pity and love, or for the one between longing and sorrow. Just as words cannot describe what I feel right now, something between envy and shame, and between compassion and disappointment.

"We move on tomorrow," Jasper announces. "We have lingered here long enough. We sell nothing camped in the wilderness. And I am bored." He accuses me, with a hard glance, of being the reason for his boredom. His jealousy of O'Neill's impetuous kiss still festers, obviously.

"Very well," Soraya says. "You are the man of the family until the doctor recovers his strength." She scoops a spoonful of liquid from the pot and holds it beneath her nose. "Hmm. It needs more amber dust, and another hour of cooking."

I stand, unable to bear the stench any longer and eager to be alone with my thoughts of sleeping draughts. It is a relief to have something to think of besides O'Neill's brazen kiss. "I am going for a walk," I declare, expecting Soraya to object.

"Night will fall soon," she says calmly. "Do not wander far. I have heard wild things growling and creeping nearby these last few nights."

O'Neill stands and brushes the dirt from the seat of his trousers. "I will go with you," he says.

"No!" I say. "I need to be alone, to think."

Jasper grunts. "I smell a lovers' quarrel. Which, by the by, smells far better than Mama's medicine. It is regrettable that you did not choose your lover more carefully, Clara. Of course, it is not too late to change your mind."

"Oh, be quiet!" I shout. I flounce away toward the woods.

"Wait!" O'Neill calls, following me.

"Leave me alone," I say. I walk faster, ducking under branches and stepping over fallen tree trunks, stumbling often in the growing darkness.

"Look, I said I was sorry," he says, close to catching up with me.

"Sometimes sorry doesn't mend things, O'Neill. You had no right!" I pull aside a branch so I can pass, and then let it go. It hits his chest with a loud crack.

"Clara," he says breathlessly. "Please stop. We must talk. You must listen."

From high in the trees comes a shriek. Seconds later, a wyvern descends, knocks O'Neill to the ground, and sits on him.

Osbert is my hero, again.

"Get off!" O'Neill shouts as Osbert licks his face. "Down, you big lout! Down, Osbert!"

If I were in a better mood, I would laugh at O'Neill's ineffectual struggling.

Finally, Osbert hops off O'Neill's body. He sits on his haunches and smiles, drool dripping from his pointy chin.

"Good boy, Osbert," I say. I rub the spot between his triangular ears and he whacks his tail against the forest floor. "At least I can still trust Osbert to behave as he should."

"It is good that he stays nearby," O'Neill says, "although he can be quite a pest." He pulls himself to his feet using a sapling for leverage. He brushes pine needles and slobber from his cheek. "We may well need a wyvern's aid very soon." He picks a beetle off my shoulder and I wince at his touch. "Clara, you must forgive me for Maren's sake. Or at least pretend to forgive me long enough for us to plan our escape."

I cross my arms over my chest. "For Maren's sake."

"Good."

"I do have an idea," I say. "If I can get into Soraya's herb cupboard, I think I can concoct a sleeping draught for Jasper and Soraya. I helped Auntie make a few doses not so long ago. But if I mix it wrong—"

"I have every confidence in you. Do not consider failing, Clara. Not now."

His compliment and the earnestness in his voice warm my whole body. I wish I could become immune to him. Quickly, I ask, "Will we take horses?"

"Yes. The two fastest. They have pledged their loyalty to me."

A rumbling growl comes from the treetops. I remember Dr. Phipps's dream monster and begin to panic, but Osbert continues happily smacking his tail up and down. If we were in danger, he would certainly alert us.

"We should go back," O'Neill says. "Or Jasper will come looking for us."

Yes, I think, *and you might be forced to kiss me again, which would only further confound my heart and send Jasper into a jealous rage.* I turn my attention to my wyvern. "I will see you again soon, Osbert," I say. I kiss his cool reptilian jowl. It is the only kiss I will be doling out today. I hope. I think of Jasper and I shudder.

Briskly walking side by side, O'Neill and I follow the vile scent of Soraya's medicine back to the camp.

We are within sight of the wagon when O'Neill grabs my hand and says, "We do need to talk. I know you are still angry with me, and I do not like it."

"You ought to have thought of that *before* you made me angry," I say, pulling my hand out of his grasp. "Sometimes you are as bad as Jasper, taking liberties with no regard for the consequences. With no regard for anyone's feelings but your own."

I run ahead of him into the circle of firelight. Jasper eyes me hungrily as I straighten my skirt and tuck a stray strand of hair behind my ear. Am I any safer here than in the woods with wild beasts and the enigmatic, exasperating O'Neill? A blush heats my face like the hottest summer sun, and I feel like I am a living example of the expression "out of the frying pan and into the fire."

Nestled amongst plump cushions and down-filled coverlets, Dr. Phipps dozes as Jasper and O'Neill drive the wagons northward. It is early June, and even with every window of the wagon thrown open, the atmosphere within is close to stifling. Soraya, wearing only a cotton shift, beats the air with a fan made of brightly colored feathers. Beads of sweat dot her forehead and upper lip.

Constrained by my innate modesty, I refuse to lounge about in my undergarments. Jasper can clearly view us through the open window, and Auntie always warned Maren and me not to tempt men by revealing "too many secrets." Besides, I know full well that Jasper needs no temptation at all. Since O'Neill's foolish kiss, Jasper has made plain his desire for me.

Consequently, I am drenched in perspiration, short of breath, and short of temper.

Maren is unbothered by the heat; I imagine she dreams of tropical waters as she sways within her jar.

Whenever Dr. Phipps moans, Soraya dabs his forehead with a damp cloth and sings softly, foreign songs with foreign words, but unmistakably songs of love. From time to time, she puts a cup to his lips and he swallows some of her malodorous medicine. She has dosed him with it a hundred times, and yet he seems neither better nor worse.

He sleeps most of the day away, much like Maren. And in his case, it seems a good thing. He does not bellow, threaten, or terrorize. He does not create lies to enslave people, or dole out poisoned (or unpoisoned) tea.

In fact, Jasper, O'Neill, and I have not tasted the doctor's Beloved Bondage tea in days. And none of us have suffered for lack of it. Jasper has not mentioned it once, but surely he must have noticed by now.

"The medicine is gone," Soraya says as she taps the little bottle against the rim of the cup. "I will make more tonight."

"Is it helping?" I ask, wishing she would doze off so I could search her cabinets for the ingredients to make the sleeping draught. But her naps have become exceedingly rare since her husband fell ill.

"Of course," she says. "Without it, he would have faded away by now, into the world between life and death. And then, one day, the gods would choose his next path. Perhaps leading into the everlasting pleasures of paradise, perhaps not. The gods are such temperamental beings. On one day, they might deem a man worthy of paradise, but on another they might decide the very same man should return to earth as a dung beetle. You simply cannot predict these things."

"Oh," I say. Her religion does not sound comforting in the least.

Soraya rests her head against the wall and resumes the fluttering of her feathered fan. "I have heard you say that your aunt is a healer. Tell me about her."

To pass the time and to distract myself from the unbearable heat, I decide to answer her. "Auntie Verity is kindness itself," I say. "She is very old and very wise. Her hair is as gray as ashes, and she wears it in a knot, speared with a pencil in case she needs to jot down a note or receipt. She is never without an apron. Her favorite is printed with tiny violets, and it has been mended so many times that it is practically quilted." I smile, picturing her using the edge of that apron to wipe batter from the corner of my four-year-old mouth.

"Go on," Soraya says. She takes a tasseled pillow from the floor and places it behind her back.

"Auntie has beautiful hands. Long, tapered fingers with elegant nails, each with a perfect crescent moon at its base, each as pink as the inside of a seashell—despite her endless gardening and yarn dyeing. They are not young-looking hands, but they are lovely. They have led me through forests, soothed me when I was hurt or afraid, and kneaded the bread for our table. They have picked plants and herbs that saved many a life, and they have delivered so many babies that Auntie has lost count."

I am thinking of Maren as I speak, and of all the things Auntie has done for *both* of us. But I will not tell Maren's story to Soraya. I would never entrust her with the tale of the seashell, the stork, and the apple tree. That tale is as sacred to me as Soraya's fickle gods are to her.

"You left her behind," Soraya says. "In my culture, we do not abandon our elders."

"Auntie knows I had to leave to save Maren's life," I say. "She knows I will return to her as soon as I can. I would be home now if your husband had not interfered with our journey."

She opens her eyes and scowls. "Speak carefully, Clara. My husband is my king, and I will not have you speak ill of him."

"I beg your pardon," I say—to pacify her, not because I regret what I said.

"Tell me of your sister," she says, her voice calm again.

"She loves water. She always has. And one day, she began to change into a mermaid." I stop, unwilling to share the intimate details of my sister's story with someone who has taken advantage of her.

"How did this happen? Did your aunt put a spell on her? Did someone else curse her?"

"I don't know. Perhaps she angered the water sprites of our mountain springs. Perhaps they were jealous of her beauty. They are hideous little creatures, the Llanfair spring sprites." There. I can spin a yarn as well as Scarff if I try.

"Ah," Soraya says. "The water spirits of my country are also vain creatures, and dangerous."

"You understand, then," I say.

"Magical creatures are not to be toyed with," she says. She yawns daintily and closes her eyes.

I stare at her, puzzled and a little angry. Is this what she truly believes? How dare she say such a thing, when she herself toys with Maren's life? Or does she only do what the doctor decrees, whether she thinks it right or wrong? I want to shake her, to make her understand the incongruity of her words and actions. To make her consider the consequence of her "toying with" my mermaid sister.

But she has fallen asleep, and now Dr. Phipps is staring at me with vacant eyes.

I get up and move out of his line of sight. He does not attempt to follow me with his eerie gaze. For that, I am thankful.

As soon as Soraya's snoring commences, I hasten to the cabinet that houses her medicinal herbs. Fortunately, it stands behind the doctor's couch—were Soraya to awaken, she might not see me right away.

I slide open the drawers and pull out little bottles, looking for the proper labels. White pennythorn leaf, root of flameweed, dried doe's milk, petals of chamomile. I drop the bottles into my skirt's pockets. But although I search every drawer, I do not find the scarlet truffle powder necessary to complete the concoction.

Dr. Phipps cries out in his sleep and Soraya stirs. I return to my place on the floor before she opens her eyes.

I will wait for another chance to continue my pilfering.

Of course, more waiting is not at all what I would wish for.

Chapter Twenty-Five

The patrons chatter excitedly as they leave the showground. They have seen a fire juggler, listened to a captivating songstress, watched a magician make a scandalously dressed girl disappear into thin air, and danced to the music of a devilishly handsome violinist. They have purchased cures for stomach ailments, women's troubles, gout, and consumption. They have bought balms to treat baby rashes and bug bites. They have stared in wonder at the jarred eyes of Egyptian pharaohs and a braid of Saint Catherine's hair (strands of corn silk woven together three days ago by a bored Jasper). And they have visited a real, live mermaid.

If they had seen the wyvern lurking in the top of a nearby hemlock tree, they would not be quite so jolly.

Outside the gallery tent, I wave to Osbert, knowing his keen eyes will see me even in the pale, flickering light of the torches outlining the camp. Tonight, there is no moon.

A blanket falls over my shoulders. "If Auntie saw that gown, she'd faint," O'Neill says.

I gather the blanket around myself like a cape. "If I saw myself in this gown, *I'd* likely faint," I say. "I have made every effort to avoid mirrors and reflective surfaces."

"All those poor farm lads will have indecent thoughts for weeks because of you."

I scowl. "I do not find that especially amusing, O'Neill," I say. "I already feel guilty for wearing such a revealing dress. You know it was not my choice."

A look of genuine repentance appears on his face. "I am sorry, Clara. I only meant to tease you a little. I forgot how ladylike you are. How Scarff always remarked upon your perfect manners."

"I will forgive you since you brought me this blanket to make up for my lack of fabric." I smile at him, and he repays me in kind.

"You do look beautiful in that ruby color, though."

"Thank you," I say, wishing the butterflies in my stomach would cease their fluttering. The memory of O'Neill's kiss makes my knees weak. Why are his eyes so blue? Why must he stand so close?

I look about us to make sure we are alone before changing the subject. "I have all but one ingredient for the draught," I whisper.

"Good," he says. "The horses are ready, and I have set aside a large tin bucket with a lid for Maren. It will have to do."

"Yes," I say. "She is fading fast. Whatever Soraya put in her water is no longer working to keep her well. We must get her to the ocean quickly."

"Trust me," O'Neill says. "I will get us away from this show and save Maren. I have promised, and I promise again."

"I hope so," I say. "With all my strength."

From across the camp, Jasper shouts for O'Neill.

"Duty calls," he says. "Jasper needs me to check the horses' shoes. And *you* need to change your clothes." He gives me one last crooked smile and walks away.

He takes my silly heart with him. I have lost all control of the blasted thing.

Rain patters on the roof of the wagon like the dancing feet of a hundred happy elves. A rumble of thunder vibrates the floor beneath my thin pallet. I roll over and wonder if Jasper and O'Neill's tent is keeping the rain out. I am glad that Soraya has insisted that I sleep in the wagon with her and the doctor.

"To safeguard your virtue," she said after my first night of performing as magician's assistant. "The men of the town must not have an easy path to you. Sleeping alone in a tent offers you no protection at all." I think that even she finds my costume vulgar—yet she does not offer me a different one.

Through the tiny gaps in the window shutters, I watch lightning flicker. I count the seconds between the bursts of illumination and the thunderclaps. And finally, sleep overtakes me.

A huge stork leads me through the sky. Up and down, with elegant slowness, his wings move through the warm air. I follow him on weaker, smaller wings. My neck aches from the weight of its burden. I look down and see, dangling from a length of pink ribbon, an enormous conch shell. As I watch, it grows larger and larger until its weight pulls me into a rapid downward spiral toward the boiling sea. I open my beak to scream, but no sound escapes before I plunge into the churning waters.

With a gasp, I awaken. The storm has passed, and the early birds are twittering gaily just outside the wagon. I lift one arm to examine it. No feathers have sprouted. Not this morning. That dream will not come true today.

I push my blankets aside and dress in my work clothes. While buttoning my shoe, I glance toward Soraya's cot. She is gone. On the couch, the doctor snores lightly.

Heart pounding, I hurry to the cupboard where Soraya stores her prized spices. My hand trembles as I examine jars and packets; Soraya has forbidden me to touch these precious seasonings, and she could appear at any moment.

Finally, I spy a thumb-sized vial of crimson dust. It is unmarked, so I uncork it and hold it to my nose. Its earthy scent and unusual color give me reason enough to believe that I have found the scarlet truffle powder I need for my potion.

Dr. Phipps stirs, and I look his way. He stares at me blankly, like a sleepwalker. Although I do not think he truly sees me, I smile at him and close the cupboard as if I am only doing my regular chores.

My smile is genuine, for I hold in my hand the key to our escape.

I need only the chance to boil the ingredients over the fire, and then the draught will be ready.

I wonder how Soraya and Jasper will like *my* special tea.

Before I go to make breakfast, I duck into the gallery tent to check on Maren. Her color is more gray than pearly, and her cheeks have hollows that were not there yesterday. Her eyes are closed.

I think she may be dead.

My heart sinks and beats wildly at the same time. But then she flicks the end of her dull-scaled tail, giving evidence that she is still alive.

The apprehension I feel for my sister is more disturbing than any nightmare.

Maren is alive, but she is dying, and we cannot afford to wait any longer to take her home.

"Without the sleeping draught, it is too risky," O'Neill says when I tell him we must leave immediately. I follow him into the wagon and watch as he kneels and rifles through a box of supplies labeled "horse treatments." He chooses a well-used-looking tin of something and then stands, facing me. "Once you finish preparing it properly, we will go without delay."

"When will I get the chance to cook it? It could be days. A week. Maren is dying, O'Neill. How many times have you promised to rescue her? And now, when she is at her most desperate, you will not try? Well, I will save her myself." My panic is leaking out in bitter accusations, but I can no longer control myself. I cannot stop the racing of my pulse or the feeling that I am about to suffocate, nor can I stem the flow of words I will likely be sorry for later.

He takes me by the shoulders. His fingers pinch my collarbones uncomfortably.

"Let go, O'Neill," I demand. "You are a coward and a liar. Let me go!"

"Not until you promise to wait. Just a little longer, please, Clara. You would risk three lives and lose them all if you acted now. Jasper suspects we are plotting and he is keeping a close eye on me—and the horses. We would not get half a mile on foot before he'd track us down and kill us. Except for Maren, of course. He would take her back and let her finish dying inside that jar, getting all the glory he could from her, for as long as she lasted."

"We could ask Osbert to attack him."

"Jasper is wearing a pistol. Osbert is not bulletproof."

"Speak to the horses, then. Or your bird friends. Surely they could help."

"They are simple creatures, Clara. They can fetch and carry, but they're not able to understand complex plans. And they don't deserve to be put in danger any more than Osbert does. Besides, their laws do not permit them to commit murder at any humans' behest."

"Then she will die. And I will die with her, or forever regret not trying to save her."

"You will not die. You'll wait, and we will save her together."

Tears blur my vision. "We will not save her. The truth is, it is too late. All our plans are foolish and futile. We have failed her. *I* have failed her by wishing when I ought to have been *doing*."

Before I can stop myself, I am weeping on O'Neill's shoulder, clutching his shirt with both hands. He pats my back gently. "Clara, Clara," he soothes. "Please do not give up. Remember what Auntie always says? We must let hope carry us when our hearts' legs fail us. Or something like that."

Through my tears, I laugh at his clumsy misquotation.

He wipes my face with his fingertips. "You see how we take turns despairing and then encouraging one another? Neither of us could have come this far alone."

He has that look in his eyes, the boy-stupefied-by-mermaid look. But he is looking at me.

"O'Neill!" Jasper shouts from the far side of the camp. "Are you bringing the liniment for the horse or not? I haven't got all day!"

"Coming," O'Neill says. He kisses my forehead in a most brotherly, most comforting way. "Hope, Clara. And be patient for just a little longer."

He leaves me with a hundred questions whirling in my mind.

I wish I could answer even a handful of them, and that the answers would be good and pleasing and peaceful. I wish that wishing would bring the best ending to us all, with the least amount of suffering.

Soraya calls me to the wagon and I hasten to serve her. Very soon, I will no longer be her servant. I will give O'Neill one or two more days, and then I must act—with or without him.

CHAPTER TWENTY-SIX

I wish that we would travel east, toward the ocean. Instead, Jasper insists upon a northward route. His fondest dream, he says, is to perform for the Eskimos. If he is joking, I cannot tell.

But before we go to Canada, Jasper says we must make a detour to call upon the apothecary who bottles Dr. Phipps's formulas. Record sales have depleted the show's supplies. Jasper gives the credit for this to "our good-luck mermaid."

Another steaming day oppresses those of us who must ride inside the wagon. I am most seriously considering stripping to my chemise—and then huddling behind boxes so as not to provoke Jasper's lust.

Soraya naps and Dr. Phipps mumbles. I am not sure whether he is awake or asleep. Perhaps he cannot tell, either. Few of his ramblings are comprehensible, but from what I have managed to glean, he is dreaming again of the visitation of a gigantic winged monster. Sometimes he wails and cries as if the thing were eating him alive.

In her jar, Maren floats like a dead leaf, just below the water's surface. I keep my back to the jar. The sight of her rends my heart, and I cannot bear to look upon her often. If I am to lose her, I would rather remember her as she was: vibrant and sparkling, her shining hair suspended about her like a halo and her face aglow with delight, swishing her silvery-green tail. Or as my two-legged sister, riding her pony bareback and frightening the hens out of the yard with her wild yelping.

"Soraya," I whisper when she stirs. "Could you help my sister? She is not at all well. Perhaps if you made more of that liquid you first put her in?"

"I cannot help her," she says, yawning. "Sometimes they live long, and sometimes they do not. Mermaids are unpredictable. If she dies, we will find another. Eventually."

"Another? I have no other sister. I will never have another sister."

"Well, that is no fault of mine," she says, closing her eyes again.

If I were a fighter, I would beat her bloody with my fists. If I were a stork, I would stab her with my bill.

The day of travel seems endless. I poke my needle into my latest mending project and sew crooked seams that must be ripped out and restitched. And the wagon sways and squeaks, and the doctor snores, and Soraya sighs and flutters her fan back and forth, back and forth.

Through the window, I see a steeple and then a series of slate-shingled roofs. Finally, we stop, thanks be to all that is holy.

Jasper meets me as I climb down from the wagon. Or, rather, as I practically throw myself out of the wagon.

"This is Edgemere," Jasper says. "You may visit the shops on the main street. I'll be over there." He points across the street to a building marked "Apothecary, B. D. Hobart." He tosses a purse my way. I catch it and it jingles. "Buy a new dress, will you? And throw that outfit into the trash. It is not fit to be seen." He smiles as if he is doing me a great favor, as if he does not owe me a hundred dresses for all the work I have done for him and his parents.

I summon a polite smile. "Thank you," I say. I will use the manners Auntie taught me, no matter how rudely Jasper speaks to me.

"Just be back here in two hours. Don't make me come looking for you." His tone is jovial, but as he walks past me, he squeezes my arm hard enough to bruise it. I do not mistake his meaning.

O'Neill speaks to the horses in front of the small wagon, praising their diligence and promising them treats. We exchange a solemn glance. I believe he is silently reminding me to be patient, and not to stir up trouble with our captors.

Clutching the purse, I make my way along the street. Beebe's General Store, The Fern Hotel and Tea Room, and the offices of The *Edgemere Gazette* occupy one side, and on the opposite side are The Red Hedgehog Tavern, a bakery, and a dressmaker's shop. The tea room tempts me greatly, but Jasper was right about my attire; my bodice is stained and worn thin in spots, and no two buttons are exactly alike. Not at all fit to be seen.

Inside the dressmaker's shop, Mrs. Smith, the elderly proprietress fusses over me. She carries no ready-made garments, but offers me something she has just finished fashioning for herself—a practical and modest green dress embellished with black lace. With nimble fingers that belie her age, she quickly tailors it to fit me.

I insist on paying her all the money Jasper gave me—a very generous sum, indeed.

"Wait, dear," Mrs. Smith calls as I step into the street. "You have left your things behind."

"My employer said to throw them away," I say. "Would you mind?"

"Not the item in the pocket, surely," she says, raising an eyebrow.

The dagger! How could I have forgotten it? "Oh, my," I say. "Forgive my absentmindedness."

She beckons me back to the private changing room. "I have not seen such a thing in many years," she says. She closes the door and takes the scabbard out from beneath the pile of my discarded garments. "May I examine it?"

"Yes," I say, puzzled by her look of amazement.

She holds the blade in a beam of sunlight and turns it slowly. "How did you come upon such a treasure?"

"A friend gave it to me. Even so, I would not call so plain a thing a treasure."

She gasps. "You do not know?"

I shake my head.

"It is a healing blade. What it cuts, it mends. It is older than the mountains, made by the pixies in the Old Country." She sheathes it and places it in my hands as if it was a holy relic. "Take great care of it, my dear. I have a feeling in my old bones that you will have need of it soon. But be wise, for it may only be used once." She pats my cheek as Auntie used to. "You must be a very special girl to have been given such a thing."

I hold the dagger in front of me, unsure what to do with it.

Mrs. Smith points to my hip. "Your dress has deep pockets. I never make one without them."

The scabbard easily slides into a pocket. The skirt falls just so, hiding its presence. "You are a great seamstress," I say. "And very kind."

She beams with pride. "Hurry along now, dear. It is getting late."

The church bell tolls five as I reach the wagons.

"Miraculous," Jasper says from the large wagon's doorway. "You should have a new dress every day."

"Who's flirting now?" O'Neill says from behind me.

"Shall we duel at dawn?" Jasper asks. "Swords or pistols?"

"Definitely swords," O'Neill says. "But Clara will most likely win."

"Touché!" Jasper says with a chuckle as he hops to the ground. "The road beckons, my children."

As O'Neill passes me, he whispers, "You look very pretty, Clara."

My face heats. I blush more deeply as I berate myself for blushing too much. Just what I need, I think, to feel even hotter when I am about to climb back into an oven of a wagon.

The next evening, in an odd little town that Jasper says is entirely populated by shoemakers, the show goes on. I swear it will be my last—and Maren's. Whether I find time to cook the sleeping draught or not, tomorrow morning, or perhaps afternoon, we will leave the Phipps family behind. I vow this to myself, over and over. I will tell O'Neill of my plans tonight if I find a way to speak to him alone. He will object, but I will not be swayed this time. I must take this last chance to save my sister's life.

After the show, an almost impossibly tall cobbler sidles up to me. (I know he is a cobbler because he forgot to remove his tool belt before leaving his shop.) With the air of a frightened rabbit, he looks down into my face, and then at my boots. He is polite enough to resist staring at my scanty costume.

"Pardon me, miss," he says. "If I might measure your lovely foot, I would reward you with a pair of fine shoes before the sun rises."

"That is very kind," I reply. "But I have no money to pay you."

"I would do it for the joy of it," he says quietly. "And for a single strand of your beautiful hair."

"Clara!" O'Neill shouts. "You are needed in the wagon. Urgently!"

"I am sorry," I say to the timid cobbler. New shoes—shoes made for my feet rather than Soraya's—would have been most useful on my upcoming journey. "Sorry."

Gripped with fear, I climb the steps into the wagon. Is Maren worse? Is she *dead*?

"What is it?" I ask.

"You were in grave danger," O'Neill says. "That shoemaker's wares cost a terrible price."

I laugh. "You are mistaken. He said he'd make them for the joy of doing so."

"And a strand of your hair. And with that exchange, you would be bound to him and his kind forever."

"Is that some kind of ancient shoemaker marriage ritual?" I think O'Neill is making a fool of me again.

"He is of elven blood. And so are most of the citizens of this mountain. Jasper knows it, and he brought us here anyway. He endangers us all."

Soraya speaks from the dark corner where she holds vigil over the doctor. "Jasper came here because I asked him to. These elven folk grow the seven-needle root I need to cure Dr. Phipps."

"And has Jasper procured it?" O'Neill asks. "Or shall we spend the night here and risk our mortal souls?"

"Neelo, child! How dramatic you are!" She laughs. "So suited for the stage!" She leans back and languidly flutters her fan. "Yes, Jasper has the root. Go strike the show and hitch the horses, and we can flee this place that turns you into a scared little boy." She giggles behind her fan. I suspect that she has been drinking wine from the cabinet behind her.

"I will change out of my costume and help you," I say to O'Neill. Through the open window, I glimpse Osbert in the treetops, and I wonder if he would have swooped down to save me from the shoemaker if O'Neill had not intervened. Who can know the mind of a wyvern?

"I must speak to you," I whisper to O'Neill as I brush past him.

But Jasper joins us and keeps close as a shadow until the last item is packed. And then he commands O'Neill to take the driver's seat of the smaller wagon. It seems that Jasper is as anxious to leave the elven folk as O'Neill is. So we set out in the dark, traveling slowly by the light of the moon.

Come morning, I will tell O'Neill of my plan to rescue Maren.

The moon is now on her slow slide down the sky. Morning will come very, very soon, and someday I will tell the tale of this new day: the day of our escape.

I wish I could say for certain that my tale will be a good one.

CHAPTER TWENTY-SEVEN

The river rushes by, tumbling over rocks and around the skeleton of a fallen tree. The sun hides behind a veil of clouds. Near where I sit on the stony beach, Soraya boils her latest pot of miracle cure. This one stinks worse than any of its predecessors. Stewed seven-needle root smells like an angry skunk bathed in sulfur.

The water moves fast. Would it carry my sister to the sea if I asked it to? She weighs very little and would be so willing to ride its currents. She would cause it no trouble at all.

I hug my knees to my chest. Grief has its fingers about my throat and I can barely breathe. Should I place Maren's body in the river? At least then she would be free. And perhaps she would make it to the ocean. Perhaps she would live.

If she remains ensconced in that jar, she will, undoubtedly, die before the week is out.

Can I make it to the ocean in time? Is it possible?

For a moment, O'Neill's spicy Christmas scent eclipses the stench of Soraya's medicine. He crouches next to me. "Something is going to happen tonight," he whispers. "I think we will take our leave." His gaze is fixed on a heron standing on twig-like legs in the shallow water near the opposite shore. I study his face, admiring the shape of his nose, the color of his eyes, the certainty of his jaw, the little heart-shaped birthmark on his chin.

"How do you know?" I watch the heron dip its bill into the dark water.

"It is a feeling I have. An intuition the gypsies taught me to respect."

"What should we do?"

"Nothing, for the moment. Things will unfold, I think, without our interference."

"I was planning to go today, to take Maren, no matter what," I say. "But I trust you. I will do as you say, as long as it is *today*." In the trees above the heron, I glimpse the wing of my pet wyvern. "Osbert," I whisper.

"I see him," O'Neill says. He picks up a small round stone and rolls it in his hand, and then he makes it disappear. "Clara," he says softly, somehow making the two syllables of my name as beautiful as any sonnet.

I remember his kiss.

"What?" I do not know what else to say. My knees begin to tremble and I hug them more tightly. The memory of his mouth touching mine is the strongest memory I have, so strong that it makes my chest ache.

"If we fail, if we die here—"

"You must not say that," I say. "It is bad luck."

"Well, then," he says.

"Come, Neelo," Soraya beckons from behind us. "Come hold this bottle for me so I may fill it."

He looks into my eyes and I think he must see my soul. He must know what I have tried so hard to deny. He must know that I love him beyond all reason.

But he stands and leaves me without another word.

Dinner is over, the dishes have been wiped clean in the river, and Soraya has gone into the wagon to tend to the doctor.

With O'Neill's help, Jasper sets Maren's jar beside the fire, regarding me as though he expects me to repay him with adoration. In the firelight, Maren looks like a cursed and feverish fairy-tale creature. Her eyes are glassy and she lies very still upon her bed of pearls.

I hang the kettle over the fire, pretending to make tea. With my back to Jasper, I empty my packet of mixed herbs into the water. I pray that this concoction does not betray me by creating a foul stench. And I wait for it to boil.

I turn and catch O'Neill's eye. He nods, signaling that he has seen my furtive activity.

"Sing something, Neelo my lad. Make us swoon with your grand talents," Jasper says as he sits down on the wooden chair closest to where I stand. He reaches beneath the chair and brings out a black bottle. He uncorks it with his teeth and takes a swig. "Come sit beside me, Clara. Better yet, try my lap."

"I will sit when this tea is done," I say.

O'Neill taps on Maren's jar. "This was your favorite when we were young," he says. He sings to her as if she is the only person— or mermaid—in the world. The song is an old English ballad (or so Scarff has always claimed) about a young husband who goes to sea, promising to bring back treasures for his bride. Instead, he falls prey to a siren whose song makes him steer his ship into a whirlpool. Of course he dies, but he does so with his true love's name on his lips.

"La, that's an awful song!" Jasper says, slurring his words. "Truly dreadful."

"I never cared for that one, either," I say. Jealousy churns in my stomach. It is an ugly thing, and I hate it. But I am weary to the bone of waiting to escape . . . and of wishing O'Neill would love me, and wishing that I did not love him.

O'Neill shrugs. "Maren adored that song when we were six. She used to demand to hear it ten times in a row."

I remember all too well. "Scarff always refused and called her a rascal, but she never failed to charm him into singing it again," I say. The pleasant memory eases my jealous heart—a little.

Jasper hands the bottle to O'Neill. He plugs the hole with his thumb and pretends to drink. He wipes his mouth on his sleeve for good measure. O'Neill passes me the bottle, and I do the same.

"We shall be famous," Jasper announces. "The three—I mean, the four of us. You two and me and our mermaid. We shall perform before the crowned heads of Europe. Queens will fall in love with me, and you can have the duchesses, Neelo. And Clara here will wear fancy gowns and rub our tired feet with her hair."

Jasper is definitely drunk. I shove the bottle back into his grasp.

If he drinks himself into unconsciousness, we will not need the sleeping draught. I question O'Neill with my eyes. He motions for me to remain still. I hear the mixture bubbling in the kettle behind me. In another minute, it should be ready.

"Neelo, my lad," Jasper continues. "You should quit dilly dallying and marry Clara. Because if you don't, one of these nights . . . one of these long, lonely nights, I am going to make a dishonest woman of her. And after just one night with me, she will never want anyone else but me. Especially not you, juggler boy."

"You are a pig, Jasper!" I glare at him and clench my hands into fists at my sides.

"See? She is a tigress, Neelo. A tigress who wants taming." Jasper sucks on the wine bottle like a calf at an udder.

Let O'Neill serve the tea. I have heard enough. "I am going to bed," I say, immediately regretting my choice of words.

"Is that an *invitation*? And is it for Neelo or for me?" Jasper doubles over with laughter.

O'Neill springs to his feet. "That is no way to speak to a lady," he says. His nostrils flare and I suspect he wants to punch Jasper as much as I do. But he breathes deeply and says, "Why don't you get us some of that tea, Clara? We are out of wine and Jasper seems to still have a thirst."

"Tea? Bah! I will get more wine," Jasper says.

I lift the kettle and fill Jasper's favorite mug with reddish brown liquid. "But I made this for you, Jasper," I say. I step close to him and offer the drink, smiling as sweetly as I can. "Try it, for me?"

He takes the mug and pulls me into his lap at the same time. "Ah," he says. "I feel like a king. I am a king." He swallows the draught in a few loud gulps. I try to stand but his arm holds me to him like a vise.

"What was that you said before, Clara? About going to bed?" His breath is hot on my neck.

O'Neill has panic and confusion in his eyes. "More tea?" he says.

"La, no! Terrible stuff, that was." Jasper stands with me in his arms, cradling me close to his chest. "You finish it, O'Neill. I have better plans."

"Put me down," I say. "Please, Jasper."

"Why would I?" he says. "You have teased me long enough."

"Just for a few moments. I want to wear the red costume for you. Let me put it on, and I will dance for you."

He sets me down. He sways a little, putting his hand on my shoulder to steady himself. "Hurry, then," he says. "Come to my tent. Or I will come and find you, little vixen."

I walk to the wagon, hoping against hope that Jasper will topple like a tree before I get inside.

My right foot is on the lowest step when I hear an unearthly moan and a resounding crash from inside the wagon. I step back.

"Sit down, my love!" Soraya's voice pleads. "You are unwell!"

Another crash. The sound of glass breaking.

"You have poisoned me, you faithless whore!" Dr. Phipps bellows.

"No! You are better now! See how your strength has returned!"

Soraya backs out the door and stumbles down the four steps. I move out of her way.

"Calm yourself, my love. You need to rest." Her eyes are wild with fear. "I think your new medicine has disagreed with you, my darling. Hush, now."

Jasper's legs buckle and he sits down hard in the dirt, watching his frantic mother and yawning like a spectator at an uninspiring show.

O'Neill pulls me farther away from Soraya as the doctor emerges. His face is purple, streaked with red. Bright blood flows freely from a gash above one eyebrow. His rumpled clothes hang from his emaciated body. His hands are curved into claws.

Soraya hums a shaky lullaby and steps backward, arms extended to ward off her husband's approach.

With a springing leap, Dr. Phipps catches her by the throat. He growls as he crushes her delicate neck between his dusky hands.

O'Neill rushes toward them, and at that moment, a gunshot rends the air.

As if tripped, O'Neill tumbles forward, knocking Soraya and the doctor to the ground. And I scream.

"Stay back, Clara," Jasper says. He moves toward his fallen parents and O'Neill, still clutching the gun.

"O'Neill!" I cry. My feet refuse to move.

"Shut up or I'll add both your names to my collection." Jasper says through clenched teeth.

The names on his leg. They are not the names of his father's victim's. *They are the names of Jasper's kills.*

Jasper uses the toe of his boot to roll O'Neill off Soraya's still body. O'Neill moans, and I see blood seeping from his shoulder. But he is alive!

The speed at which Dr. Phipps pushes Soraya from his chest and gets to his feet is nothing short of supernatural. His fists pummel Jasper's face and neck before Jasper has a chance to raise his gun. The force of a blow to his ribs causes Jasper to drop the gun and collapse onto the ground.

"How do you dare, son?" Phipps rages. "How do you dare attempt to murder *me*?"

From where he has fallen, Jasper lifts his empty hands in surrender. "I shot O'Neill to save you, Papa," he says quickly. "He has a knife! He would have stuck you with it!"

Dr. Phipps kicks Jasper in the side and then in the head. Jasper curls into a ball and whimpers.

"After all that I have done for you!" Phipps shouts. "After all I have given for you!" He staggers toward the fire. "For you, my son, I created the most spectacular shows! I gave you all that you asked! I washed the blood from your guilty hands time after time, and I gave you everything!"

Phipps pulls a blazing branch from the fire. "Enough is enough," he proclaims to the stars. "Enough!" He lifts the branch above his head and brings it down upon Maren's jar. The glass shatters and the water floods out, and Maren lies helpless on spilled pearls and glass shards. Her mouth is open in the shape of a scream. Her body flops like a beached fish's.

"No," I cry, "no!" She must not die like this, alone and afraid, suffocating for want of water.

"The show is over, son!" Dr. Phipps shouts as he wobbles and swerves his way toward the wagons. He brandishes the makeshift torch and sets the large wagon ablaze with it before tossing it through the open door of the small wagon. "By the flames of Hell, I disown it and you, Jasper! The devil take you both! You were more his son than mine."

As the doctor paces and rants about demons and betrayals, flames engulf the wagons, roaring and crackling and sending black smoke into the starry sky.

I rush to Maren and scoop up her doll-sized body. "Maren, Maren," I say desperately. She grips my arm with a tiny hand and shuts her eyes. "You must not die, sister. Please hold on."

I hurry to a bucket of water near the campfire, and I set Maren inside. It is a tight fit, but for now it must suffice.

Carrying the bucket tight against my breast, I run to a cluster of bushes and hide it under the lowest branches. "Wait for me," I say to Maren. One tiny pearl rolls down her sunken cheek. "O'Neill is hurt, and I must go back for him. Are you listening, Maren? Do not die, sister. Rest and wait for us to return. Understand?"

She nods.

I run. The flames leap above us, tongues of fire trying to lick the stars from the heavens. Dr. Phipps's maniacal laughter sends chills through my body—but it occurs to me that I am not at all afraid.

I am beyond fear's reach. I will do what I must to save O'Neill.

I run past Jasper, who's still rolled up like a scared hedgehog, muttering. My draught has not worked, after all. No wonder Auntie found me a frustrating student.

Phipps grabs Soraya by the hair and drags her along the ground. She moans faintly as her veil slips off and her beautiful yellow sari snags on sharp stones. Between her breasts, like a hideous flower, a bloodstain blossoms. The bullet that pierced O'Neill must have passed through his body and into hers.

"Look, woman," Phipps says as he yanks her into a sitting position. "Your life is in flames, ruined by your treachery and your son's wickedness!" He looks down at her then, with the smug face of a pitiless conqueror. But his whole aspect changes when he sees the spreading blood. He is transformed from vanquisher to vanquished in the blink of an eye. "My darling Soraya," he cries as he falls to his knees. "My love!" He draws her limp body into his arms and covers her with kisses. Deep, heaving sobs reduce him to a shuddering heap.

"O'Neill." I crouch beside him and gently pat his pale cheek. He opens his eyes. "Come," I whisper. "We must get away."

"The doctor is mad," O'Neill says as I haul him to his feet. "The seven-needle root has turned his brain."

"And you are wounded," I say. "Now be quiet and come along." He takes a halting step, leaning heavily on me.

"Where do you think you are going?" Jasper says from behind us. I turn. His gun is pointed at my head.

"Please," I beg. "Let us go. The show is over, and you do not need us anymore."

"Oh, but I do need you. I will make a new show: The Great Jasper and Company. But if you would prefer not to join me, O'Neill and the mermaid's names will go here," he says, pointing to his left thigh. "And I will put your name here, Clara darling." He pats his right thigh. "So that even in memoriam you shall be parted from your sister and your lover. It is your choice to make. I do not wish to kill you, truly, but if you insist on opposing me, you will leave me no other option."

O'Neill's body goes limp as he faints. Unable to support his weight, I slump to the ground, settling him next to me as carefully as I can. I look up at Jasper. Around his throat hangs a very familiar gold locket and chain. "That is Maren's locket," I say, scrambling to my feet.

"Yes, and inside the locket is the eye-stone we used to track you, so that we could possess the mermaid. Mama knew from the first time she saw Maren that she would become a valuable commodity. She sold the eye-stone to Maren's stupid suitor, and the rest is, as they say, history." His grin is pure evil.

"Did you set fire to our caravan?" I ask, my voice trembling with anger and disgust.

"It was a shame to destroy that splendid conveyance. But I did rescue you, didn't I? You should be grateful. Could you show me gratitude, Clara? Could you try to love me?" His gun is still aimed between my eyes; his expression is one of yearning mingled with madness. "I adore you, Clara. You have bewitched me. If only you would allow me to teach you the deep secrets of the night, you would forget all that was before. We could begin a new and exciting life together. What do you say, Clara?"

"I say you should go to the devil, Jasper Phipps."

I hear the whoosh of wings, followed by a piercing shriek. Osbert's claws root themselves in Jasper's scalp, and his sharp teeth lodge in the muscles of his shoulder. The gun falls to the ground with a clatter.

"Get off!" Jasper shouts, slapping and pulling at Osbert's talons.

A shadow passes between us and the moon. The shadow of another wyvern.

I hold my breath as the great wyvern swoops lower and lower. This dragon is no house pet. He would not fit through the door of any house.

The monstrous wyvern shrieks again, and Osbert releases Jasper and moves aside. When I see the great wyvern's jaws open wide enough to swallow a horse, I squeeze my eyes shut. Cracking and crunching and gulping come from where Jasper once stood.

Shivering, I open my eyes. Jasper is gone. Vanished, as if he'd never existed. Not a scrap of clothing has been left behind. Not a shoe or a fingernail.

The big wyvern belches with satisfaction.

"Great gods above!" Dr. Phipps cries, cowering beside Soraya's lifeless body. "It has come to pass!"

Both wyverns turn and eye him. Red drool drips from the big one's bared fangs.

"Osbert, no," I say. "Your friend must not eat the doctor. Please, Osbert. I have seen enough violence."

Osbert nods at the beast and it whines in disappointment. It spreads its massive wings and lifts from the ground with a rush of wind.

"No!" Phipps cries as it circles above us. When the monster dives toward him and roars, Phipps clutches his heart and screams, "Have mercy!" And then his eyes roll back in his head and his mouth slackens. His body crumples onto Soraya's, and I know that he has joined his wife in death.

Osbert scampers over and drenches my face with kisses. He kisses O'Neill until he awakens from his faint. And then our pet wyvern unfolds his wings and takes flight, following his fellow wyvern into the night with a happy waggling of his barbed tail.

I sink to the ground beside O'Neill, and he lays his head in my lap. "My brave Clara," he says.

I do not feel brave. I feel a hundred years old and very, very tired—yet wide awake with worry. My mermaid sister sits in a shallow bucket, growing weaker by the minute, and O'Neill has been shot and can barely stand.

The smell of burnt wood and cloth and singed metal lurks about us as the wagons' contents smolder and crackle. The smoke forms wispy clouds above us, obscuring the stars and dimming the moonlight.

"The horses," O'Neill says. "I tethered them over there." He points to the east. "Just beyond that hill, in a patch of grass. If you bring them, we can leave this place. We can finally take the road to the sea." He speaks boldly, but his forehead is creased with pain.

"Yes," I say. "But first I must tend to your wounds."

With unsteady fingers, I unbutton his shirt and peel the blood-soaked fabric from his skin. "I need more light," I say. "I cannot see the wound properly." All I can see is dark blood oozing steadily from a hole in his chest. "Can you move closer to the fire?"

"If you will help me," he says. His breathing is not right. Too much blood dampens my dress as I help him stumble to the fireside.

I kneel beside him. The firelight shows me what I do not wish to see. Far too much blood. His color is wrong, his breathing ragged.

"The bullet passed through, did it not?" he says.

"Yes," I say.

"Yet I do not think I will live to see the sunrise, Clara," he says. He grips my hand.

"You will," I say.

"I must tell you some things before I go."

"You are not going," I say. I pull the dagger from my pocket and unsheathe it. "What it cuts, it mends," I say, repeating Mrs. Smith's words.

"It is a healing blade? I did not recognize it before. You must use it on Maren, not me," O'Neill says. His skin is gray now, as gray as a corpse's. "Make her a girl again. Save her for my sake. Keep my promise for me."

"The blade can only be used once," I say.

"Please, Clara. If you love me at all—if you love Maren, let her be the one to live."

How can I choose between the two people I love most?

But if I choose healing for Maren, she would still be a mermaid, for there is no dagger in the universe that can make her a girl again. This is the truth I know and believe, although O'Neill continues to reject it again and again.

In choosing Maren, I would likely lose them both, for Maren would regain her size—and without O'Neill, how could I carry her and keep her concealed until we reach the sea?

There is no choice to be made. O'Neill must live or the mermaid will surely perish.

My hand trembles as I press the blade into his wound. What if Mrs. Smith was mistaken? What if I kill my dearest friend?

He coughs and wheezes. His eyes roll back and he shudders.

I cut him, tracing the bullet hole with the razor-sharp tip of the dagger.

O'Neill whimpers, and then he is quiet and absolutely still.

CHAPTER TWENTY-EIGHT

I am certain O'Neill is dead.

I have hastened his death, and Maren's death will follow swiftly.

"I am sorry," I say. I lift his hand to my lips and kiss his cold skin. There is so much I want to say, but I do not think he will ever hear another earthly thing.

I lay his hand upon his chest, inches from the ugly, seeping hole I helped create.

The wound hisses and glows. The skin stretches to cover the wound, and all traces of blood evaporate in a pink puff of air.

A crooked smile spreads across O'Neill's face just as the moonlight breaks through the clouds of smoke.

If every joy of my life could be combined into one great joy, it would still be nothing but a shadow compared to this: my dearest O'Neill, living and breathing—and attempting to wipe away my flooding tears with his beautiful, filthy fingertips.

The dawn is dim and misty, holding all the promise of another stifling day. The horses whinny as I untie them from their posts. I am glad that O'Neill tethered them away from the camp last evening. I am glad they are not now cinders like the Phippses' many treasures.

From the six horses, O'Neill chooses Plato and Cleopatra for our journey and sells the other four to a local farmer for much less than they are worth. We then return half the money to him in exchange for saddles, blankets, a sack of salt, and his promise to bury Soraya and Dr. Phipps, "victims of an unfortunate accident."

With all of his former vim and vigor, O'Neill vaults onto the back of the piebald horse. I hand him a large bucket covered with a piece of burlap, and he receives it as the priceless gift it is. He ties a length of strong rope about his waist and the bucket and makes a good, tight knot.

"I will not lose Maren now," he says. "Not after all we have been through."

I force a smile and use the fence to climb into the saddle of the chestnut mare.

"Ready?" O'Neill asks. His face is so bright and eager that I wonder if the healing blade contained some kind of mood-lifting magic.

"Yes," I say. It is half-true. I am ready to deliver Maren to her home, but I am not ready to part with her. I will never be ready to be parted from my sister.

O'Neill commands his horse to walk, and my horse follows.

We take the road to the east.

My sister is a mermaid. She is small enough to sleep within a two-quart jar of salt water.

Yesterday, when the sun was noon-high, I bought the jar from an old woman we met along the eastward-leading road, filling it with fresh, clear water from her well and salt from her pantry. O'Neill guessed the woman's favorite song and sang it through three times, making her laugh and cry simultaneously. For this, she gave us a loaf of warm bread and a thick slab of cheese. As we left, she asked O'Neill to marry her. He declined, of course. "Alas," he said sweetly, "My heart is not mine to give."

Today, the horses carry us as if we are no trouble at all, as if they are merely going where they please. O'Neill rides Plato with the grace of a prince, and I manage not to fall off Cleopatra's muscular back.

O'Neill keeps Maren's jar tied to his body as we travel. He talks to her often, although she rarely responds. He sings to her until his voice is hoarse. Let him cherish her while he may. She is almost home now.

The soil becomes sandier with each passing mile; the trees here are not like Llanfair Mountain trees. They are silly-looking pines: skinny, knobby trunks—and branches with sparse tufts of needles. And when we stop to rest the horses, O'Neill points to the cloudless sky. I recognize the white and gray bird above us; it was Maren's favorite in Auntie's bird book, the ring-billed gull.

O'Neill loosens the knotted rope and lifts Maren's jar. "Look, Maren," he says with the radiant joy of a little boy, "A sea bird!"

Her eyelids flutter and she nods. She is so small now, just a handful. A miniature doll with tiny scales and smooth, pale, blue-gray skin.

"We will be there soon," he says. "You will finally have what you have been longing for, dearest."

She is asleep again before he finishes speaking.

My heart aches for his loss, and for mine.

We sit in the rough, dry grass beside the road. I scan the sky for sea birds while O'Neill holds Maren's jar between his knees and stares at her wistfully.

"I will ask the Sea King to release her," he says. "I will demand that he restore her to her human family."

How many times have I told him that Maren is a mermaid? That she was never meant for the land? How can I say it again? I tear a piece of grass from the ground and use it to poke at an ant.

"You will keep your sister," he says with conviction. "Even if I must trade my life for hers."

I stand and wipe the sandy soil from my dress. "Wishing gets you nothing," I say. The words are bitter on my tongue, but I do not know what else to say to him.

"I am not wishing, Clara. I am telling you the truth."

"Your truth is not *the* truth," I say. I want to lie down on the sandy ground and go to sleep for a hundred years, to wake up after the world has righted itself somehow.

"Do you regret using the healing blade on me instead of her?" he asks. "Is that why you are angry with me? Or are you still holding a grudge against me for kissing you? Will you never forgive me?"

"I am tired, O'Neill. I am tired and we are wasting time here." I walk to Cleopatra and rub her black nose. "Help me up, will you?"

He cups his hand, I step into it, and he boosts me onto the horse's back. He looks up at me and says, "I am sorry, you know. Sorry for offending you so greatly."

"I know that," I say. I close my eyes and wait for him to mount Plato. The coming end of Maren's journey fills me with dread. My heart is a tangled knot of love and hate and hope and despair. If I were a stork, life would be much simpler.

When I return to Llanfair Mountain, perhaps I will ask Auntie how to hasten my change.

As we ride, I remember the only time I have visited the ocean—the summer Maren, O'Neill, and I were seven years old.

Scarff brought us in the caravan, and he parked it behind a dune when we arrived. When the clanging and ringing of the pots and chimes all but ceased, the sound of the roaring waves filled my ears. We joined hands, three almost-siblings, and with feet slipping in the sand, ran over the dune to see the water.

We stopped, all of us as one, as soon as we could see the ocean spread out before us, vast and blue-green and powerful. The curling waves caught sunlight in their bellies before bending over it and crashing onto the beach. The sea birds called and dove above us. I remember happiness, as pure and sweet as any in my life, filling every part of me. O'Neill shouted for joy. And then Maren tore her hand free of mine and returned to the caravan in tears.

Three days we camped there. Maren, who practically lived in the pond and creek at home, refused to set foot in the ocean. All day, she sat on the dunes and wept quietly while O'Neill and I splashed and swam and collected shells.

Did she cry because she already knew that one day the ocean would take her away from us? Or did her sorrow stem from a soul-deep longing for the ocean to be her home even then?

The road before us becomes sand, and the scent of seawater taints the warm breeze. Cleopatra follows Plato, her mane ruffling in the wind. Gulls screech above us as we top a small, grassy hill, and then . . . we arrive.

It is as I remember, beautiful and untamable and wider than my vision. I grip the reins and hold back tears.

O'Neill brings Plato alongside me. After a few minutes of silence, I say, "What do we do? Should there not be a ceremony or trumpet blasts or an earthquake or something? A rainbow?"

"I don't know," he says. "I never considered this part."

I look at him from the corner of my eye. The bloodstains on his torn shirt have faded after days in the sun. His hair is dirty from travel and more thatch-like than usual. Now that we are here, everything about him says *sadness*.

On the horizon, a pod of dolphins swim together. Closer and closer they come, splashing and leaping in arcs above the water. "Dolphins," I say, pointing them out to O'Neill.

He shades his eyes with one hand and squints. "No," he says, "those are mermaids and mermen coming to meet Maren."

"My sister," I whisper.

We dismount and walk down the beach, Maren's jar still bound with rope to O'Neill's waist, as the merfolk continue to approach. Soon, we hear them singing, high and sweet and unearthly. I remember ruined sailors and glance at O'Neill. "Be careful," I warn. "They might take you in spite of your tattoo. Can it protect you from so many of them?"

But perhaps that is what he wishes for in his heart of hearts. For then he and Maren would never be parted.

A bare-chested merman, his bronze hair adorned with a wreath of sea stars, lifts a conch shell to his lips and blows. The singing ceases, the waves calm, and a towering, majestic figure moves through the crowd of merfolk. They bow as they make way for their king.

He grips a golden trident in his right hand. His hair and beard are rolling waves of silver, and his crown is a monument of gold and pearls, coral and sparkling sea glass. "Come into the water," he commands in a voice like the roaring tides. "Bring my daughter to me, for I have waited long to welcome her home."

O'Neill unties the rope and drops it onto the beach. He holds the jar to his side with one arm and offers me his other hand. Together, we wade through the fizzling foam and into the cool water. When the water sloshes at my waist, we stop.

"She is here, your majesty," O'Neill says as he raises the jar.

The mermaids gasp and cry when they see her, so small and listless in her jar. It may be too late.

"Silence!" the Sea King commands. The ocean stands still. "Bring me the jar, Varun," he says to the muscular, golden-haired prince beside him. The prince glides through the water with grace and speed and reaches out pearlescent hands to receive the precious jar.

"Wait!" O'Neill shouts. "Must you take her, your majesty? She has a family who love her, and a good life on land. Please do not take her from us."

"The jar," Varun says. "Give it to me."

"She is my daughter," the king says. His voice is a tidal wave consuming a rocky island. "She is a princess of the merfolk. She has never belonged to the human world. Her time there is done."

Varun pulls the jar from O'Neill's grasp and swims swiftly to the king.

O'Neill's hand trembles in mine. From fear or anger, I am not sure. I cannot bear to look at his face now.

The king opens the jar and pours its contents—including Maren—into his mighty palm. Then he lowers Maren into the ocean.

She disappears beneath the surface. I hold my breath, imagining her bobbing up like a dead fish. I grip O'Neill's hand desperately.

Slowly, a head of bright copper hair emerges, followed by Maren's twinkling face and alabaster shoulders. She is full-sized again, and she is perfect. Her hair cascades over her round breasts and floats about her delicate waist like metallic seaweed. She laughs with the sound of waves caressing a sandy shoreline, and the merfolk rejoice.

"Daughter," the Sea King says, his august voice heavy with emotion. She embraces him without hesitation. "How we have longed for your return!"

A dozen mermaids rush to surround her, crowning her with coral, slipping necklaces of shells about her neck, adorning her fingers with rings, brushing her hair with jeweled combs.

"Wait!" O'Neill shouts above the joyful din. "Take me instead!"

"No, O'Neill." Maren turns to address us, and the crowd becomes silent. "You must go home and live your life. This is my true home. It always has been."

"Your friends may visit our kingdom once a year, in your month of June, during our Festival of the Great Whales," the king says to Maren. He gazes upon her with fatherly love.

"She is my sister, and he is my brother," Maren says. "They have risked their lives to bring me home to you."

"They shall be rewarded," the king says. He waves his trident and a pair of sea turtles swim to us bearing a chest so large it covers both their shelled backs. "When you visit our palace, you shall receive even greater gifts for all you have done for my daughter."

"May I say good-bye to them, Father? Alone?" Maren asks.

He nods, then raises his trident again. The merfolk move toward the horizon, diving and surfacing with glad shouts and merriment. The ocean resumes its ebbing and flowing.

When she comes to embrace me, her skin is warm and emanates the fragrance of sea grasses and strange flowers, salt and seashells. There is weight to her, and strength. She is whole again—healthy and happy.

"I will miss you," I say into her ear. "Every day, I will miss you."

"And I will miss you. Never was there a better sister, or a braver one."

She releases me and takes O'Neill into her arms. "If only you had been born in a seashell," she says, "we could have made a home together beneath the waves."

O'Neill shakes his head. "You will find a merman to marry. You will be happy. I know it," he says with great effort. He does not wipe away the tears flowing from his eyes. They fall into the ocean to join the saltwater of the ages.

She kisses his cheek, and then mine.

And then she dives into the swelling waves and swims away.

We watch her go. We do not move until the rising tide forces us back to the shore.

CHAPTER TWENTY-NINE

O'Neill and I spread our blankets on the sand, on opposite sides of the driftwood campfire. Neither of us has spoken since Maren swam away. I lie awake and watch the stars turn above me. The ocean rolls and roars, splashes and murmurs. I cannot hear the voices of the merfolk anymore. I almost wonder if I imagined them. But if they were not real, then what has become of my sister?

Inside my heart an ocean of tears swells and crashes, yet I do not cry. I feel as if part of me is now made of sorrow, some new and tender organ that will pain me until the day I die. I know Maren is safe and well, and made beautiful in all ways. My grief is not for her but for myself—because I miss her . . . because she is missing *from* me.

No matter how many times I remind myself that I will see her again, the pain remains.

In the morning, I walk along the shore and dig up clams with a stick. I carry them in my skirt, forgoing my manners and exposing my knees to the gulls. They skitter after me, hoping I will share my breakfast with them.

I drop the clams into the pail of water I left to heat in the coals and O'Neill sits up and rubs his eyes.

Still, we do not speak.

Not as we eat, nor as we fold the turtles' treasures into the blankets, nor as we mount the horses, nor when we stop at midday to rest on a riverbank.

Unable to bear my filthy state any longer, I leave O'Neill while he is napping. I walk until I find a bend in the river where I can remove my dress in privacy. I scrub it against a smooth rock and then lay it on the beach to dry. In my chemise, I wade into the water until it reaches my neck. I wash my hair and body with my hands, and finally, I weep.

An hour later, I return to the place where I left O'Neill to find him pacing and running his hands through his dirty hair. "You would feel better after a bath," I say. "I found a good place just over there."

"Clara!" he shouts. "You frightened me. I thought you'd left."

"I'm sorry," I say. "But why would I leave you?"

"Because I failed you. I did not save Maren. I let your sister be taken by the merfolk."

"It is what she wanted. I have told you a hundred times, but you have not listened." I sit down on a boulder and lay my hands in my lap. "Now Maren is well, and she is home. And we will go to our home and live with Auntie and Scarff. Next year, we may visit Maren and hear her stories of sea horses and starfish and under-water courts." I speak to convince him *and* myself that these things are both true and good.

"Yes," he says. Only he does not sound convinced, not one bit. He sits at my feet and wraps his arms about his knees. Suddenly, he looks all of twelve years old.

"You must not blame yourself for things beyond your control, O'Neill. It is one of your most irritating faults." Through my pain, I smile at him, and he smiles back. It is like the sun coming out after a hundred days of rain.

"I was not aware that I had more than one fault," he says.

"Well, your stench is one." I wave my hand in front of my nose. "Please, for the love of mercy, go and wash yourself!"

"Just because your sister is a princess does not make you the queen," he says. He tosses a small rock at my bare foot.

And then he obeys.

The world will continue, as it has for thousands upon thousands of years. We will live without our dear Maren. We will finish growing up and we will work and play and love. The sun and moon will take turns shining, clouds will sail across the skies, and rain will wash the earth. I will touch snow and smell flowers. Perhaps someday I will have a child, and I will tell her of her mermaid auntie. Or perhaps I will become a stork and fly wherever the winds take me.

I wish I were a stork and not a girl without a sister.

In the nearby town, we use the Sea King's coins to purchase a covered wagon, clothes, horse tack, cooking supplies, food, soap, and a tent.

That night, we camp in a meadow beneath a million stars and a fat moon.

"I feel as rich as any king," O'Neill says, patting his full belly. His tone is cheerful, but his eyes are swollen and red from shedding countless tears.

"Does your wound bother you?" I ask.

"No," he says. "There is no sign of it, not even a scar to boast of."

I pour tea into two earthenware mugs. "That is good."

He looks at me strangely as I hand him his mug. "Clara?"

"Yes?"

"I promised you, in a letter brought to you by a very fine raven, that we would dance together. And the dancing Jasper forced us to do does not count."

"Drink your tea, O'Neill," I say. "Before it gets cold."

"A man must keep at least *some* of his promises." He sets his mug onto the ground, then he takes mine and sets it beside his.

"I do not want to dance," I say as he grabs my arm and pulls me away from the fireside. My heart races like a spooked pony.

He begins to hum, and steers me through the wildflowers and weeds. "Dance, Clara. Do not just clomp along."

I pull away from him. "I do not wish to dance."

Hurt and disappointment are in his eyes. Even the moonlight reveals that much. I turn my back, afraid my face will shame me by exposing my true feelings. I have surprised myself. I had thought that my grief had erased the last vestiges of my unsisterly love for him, but I love him still. I love him terribly and completely.

"Clara," he says, "why do you turn away from me?"

I do not reply.

He takes my arm and spins me around to face him again. "Do you not know?"

Gently, he lifts my chin and forces me to look into his sparkling eyes. Suddenly, I *do* know. He does not need to say the words, but (miracle of miracles!) he does.

"I love you, Clara."

"But you love Maren. That was why you tried so hard to save her," I say.

"Of course I love her. We have been together since we were babies. But I have never loved her the way that I love you. The way I have always loved you."

I shake my head. "But I saw you with her, so many times. The way you looked at her. The way she looked at you!"

"She did love me. She wanted me to marry her. Asked me more than once, bold as brass, in that way she had. I told her that

I loved her only as a sister, although she never accepted it. When I sat with her, when I held her hand, it was only to comfort her in her suffering. I would have done the same for Auntie. Or Osbert. I had planned to tell you in March—even Madame Vadoma knew—but when I arrived and saw Maren, and she demanded my attention . . . things did not go as planned."

"You kissed me," I say. "In the forest."

"That was not just for Jasper's sake, Clara. I had waited years for that moment with you."

All of my manners flee as I grab him by his shirtfront and pull him to me. I kiss him shamelessly, and long.

Finally, he steps back. With gentle fingers, he wipes the tears from my cheeks. "Come with me," he says. He leads me by the hand back into the camp.

"It's here somewhere," he says, rummaging through the crate full of the Sea King's gifts. "Ah, here it is."

He kneels before me and slips a ring onto my finger. "Will you be my wife?" he asks. The Sea King's rubies and gold glimmer in the firelight, and O'Neill's eyes reflect the flames. "After your forward behavior this evening, you must say yes."

"Yes," I say. "In the next town, at the next church." I kiss him again, and I swear I can hear the mermaids' sweet songs even though we are miles from the ocean. How can one heart be so full and so empty at the same time?

I shove him away suddenly. "O'Neill," I say, panicking. "I cannot marry you! What if I become a stork? It could happen at any time, perhaps even tomorrow."

He laughs. "You are no stork, Clara. You are no more a stork than I am an apple."

"But Auntie said a stork brought me to her. And after what happened to Maren . . ."

"It was Scarff," he says. "It was Scarff who found you and took you to Auntie."

"But Auntie cannot lie, and she said it was a stork."

"Scarff's given name is Ezra Corraghrian Scarff. *Corra-ghrian* means stork. It was his Scottish mother's family name. He found you on the steps of an abandoned orphanage."

"Why did they never tell me? All this time I have dreaded growing feathers and a bill!"

"Your story was so unromantic compared to Maren's and mine. They wanted you to feel special, too. To have some magic of your own. None of us thought you actually believed you would become a bird. How could you have kept such a worry to yourself all these years?"

"I did believe it. I was resigned to it, in fact. But I would much rather be your Clara. I have seen enough magic," I say. "And what does it matter where my journey began, as long as I end it with you?"

O'Neill takes both my hands. "I feel foolish, you know. Almost as if I ought to ask for your pardon."

"For what could you possibly require pardon?"

"I swore to save Maren and to protect you. But you were the hero, weren't you? You were the one who made me brave when I might have given up. You were the one who stood up to Jasper—without knowing Osbert would come to your aid. You used the healing blade to save me. You made sure Maren reached the ocean alive. You were your sister's hero, and you are mine. My brave, brave Clara."

A blush warms my face, and for once I do not mind. "How could I have been brave if you had not been beside me?"

"You would have been."

In silence, we watch fireflies rising up from the grass like little freely moving stars. And I think about not being a stork, about never becoming a stork. Yet I have changed. I have left childhood behind, and it is true—I have been braver than I thought I could be.

"It is all fine and good being brave," I say as the moon peeks out from behind a cloud. "But could we take turns at being the hero? It is a lot of work, you know."

"I rather like being the damsel in distress," O'Neill teases. "I was about to ask to borrow a dress."

"Never!" I shove him hard and he rolls into the grass. And we laugh as we have not laughed in months, as I never thought we'd laugh again.

CHAPTER THIRTY

With one hand, O'Neill raps the brass doorknocker against the wooden parsonage door. With his other hand, he clenches my hand. His palm is damp, and I suspect it is not from the heat of the day. Even a willing groom is likely to have nerves just before his wedding.

He knocks again, and we wait. "What if no one is at home?" I say. "Perhaps someone else in the town could marry us. A judge or a justice of the peace."

"Hello," a voice calls from behind us. We turn around to find a black-robed priest carrying a basket brimming with blueberries. "I was in the gardens and did not hear you arrive."

"Good afternoon," O'Neill says. "My name is O'Neill, and this is Clara. We would be most grateful if you'd marry us, Father." His words come out in a rush. His nervousness is most endearing.

"O'Neill, you say?" The priest grins, showing all three of his teeth. "Isn't that a wonder? *My* name is O'Neill, Patrick O'Neill, although I'm called Father Patrick by most." He brushes past us and opens the door. "Come in, come in. My housekeeper's gone away to see her son, so don't mind the dust."

He takes us to the kitchen and gives us cups of cool water and bowls of blueberries doused with cream. "Lad," he says, leaning close to O'Neill. "You put me in mind of someone."

"Perhaps we have met before. My guardian and I are traveling merchants and might have stopped here, although I do not remember it," O'Neill says. He spoons the last of the blueberries into his mouth. Cream runs down his chin, and he wipes it away with his hand.

"Glory be!" the priest says. "That birthmark! Now I know you, lad."

O'Neill fingers the heart-shaped birthmark on his chin. "I was an orphan."

"Yes. Yes, you were. It was in Virginia, my parish. Near my childhood home. And I found you under the apple tree where my brother was buried, a babe with a birthmark just like he'd had."

"Your brother Seamus," O'Neill says. "My guardian has told me the story many times. He named me O'Neill for your brother because he did not think I looked like a Seamus."

"He raised you well," Father Patrick says. "That I can see, even with these old eyes. Glory be to the Lord, who doth provide." His face is alight with happiness. "And here you are with your fine young lady, asking to be wed. I am blessed to witness this day."

Seeing the priest's joy makes my heart sing. Everything that has happened in our lives, from O'Neill's babyhood under the apple tree until now, has worked together to lead to this one perfect day.

"Will you marry us, Father?" I ask. "Today?"

"It would be quite unorthodox, without banns or special dispensation. I am sure my superiors would not approve. But how could I refuse the boy with my brother's birthmark?"

Father Patrick marries us in the parsonage garden, beneath an arbor of fragrant pale-pink roses. The gardener, his five-year-old daughter, and her crooked-tailed kitten are our witnesses. O'Neill and I exchange rings we found among the Sea King's treasures—gold bands that are perfectly sized and matched, as if the Sea King had somehow known our future. Perhaps he had.

The little girl claps when we seal our vows with a kiss, and the kitten startles and runs to hide in the hedges.

"Come here," I say to the girl. I take a pearl from my pocket, one of three I kept from Maren's jar to remember her by. "My sister gave this to me, and it is very special. Keep it so that you may always remember this happy day."

"Is it a treasure?" she asks.

"Yes," I say, "a very great treasure. It came from sadness but led to joy."

O'Neill kisses my cheek. "Mrs. O'Neill Scarff," he whispers in my ear. "You are sweet and kind as well as brave."

"I do not know if I am any of those things," I say, "but I am happy."

"Not as happy as I am."

"Do you pick a fight with me so soon? Five minutes after the wedding?"

He quiets me with a kiss. If that is how he chooses to win our arguments, so be it.

CHAPTER THIRTY-ONE

Smoke funnels out the chimney of the cottage where I was raised. Twilight is upon the mountain, and the lamplight glows golden through the windows.

How they knew we were coming, I do not pretend to know. But as the horses halt, Auntie and Scarff spill out the door and run to us. Osbert scampers at their heels, howling with wyvern delight.

Kisses and tears are exchanged in abundance.

"She is safe, our Maren?" Auntie asks, gripping my elbows.

"Safe with her Sea King father," I say. "And she is happier and more beautiful now than you could ever imagine."

"For that, I am glad," Auntie says. "And I am glad you are home safe as well."

"Hear, hear," Scarff agrees.

O'Neill lifts my hand to show them my rings. "We are married," I say, blushing as befits a bride.

"By the very priest who found me under the apple tree," O'Neill says. "That is a story you will enjoy, Scarff and Auntie."

"So young!" Auntie clucks her tongue. "But no matter. It was meant to be. We have always known it, haven't we, Ezra my love?"

Overcome with emotion, Scarff replies by gathering O'Neill and me into his arms again. His eyes and beard are wet with joyful tears. "All our children are safe and happy," he says. "Who could wish for more?"

After breakfast the next morning, O'Neill leads me to the Wishing Pool. His face shines with love and mischief.

"Look," he says. He points to the tree whose vandalized trunk has always warned us of the fruitlessness of wishing. *Someone* has changed the words.

"'*Swishing* gets you nothing'? Honestly, O'Neill!"

"Well, I couldn't leave it as it was. It was a lie. Besides, I made a solemn pledge to my true love that I would destroy it, and I could not bear to burn the poor tree down."

"It was a lie," I agree. "Sometimes wishing gets you *something*."

"Wishing got me everything," he says. "Eventually."

I dive into the deep water of the Wishing Pool, new dress and all.

Just as my sister would have done.

ACKNOWLEDGMENTS

I owe a debt of gratitude to the many dear friends who have encouraged me on this exciting journey. I could not possibly name each of you here, but I think you know who you are!

Special thanks to:

My husband, John, for putting up with me and quietly believing in me. You mean more to me than words can say.

My sweet grandmother, friend, and fellow book fanatic, Shirley Thomas. You read it first!

My wonderful parents, Tim and Shelley Selleck, for a million reasons.

Williamsport NaNoWriMo cohorts Brenda Crowell, Amanda C. Davis, Laura Rook, Kristina Solomon, and mascot Codi Zanella. Extra thanks to Amanda for being an incredible beta reader and for sharing your knowledge of weird nineteenth-century stuff.

Jenny Brown (writer's care-package queen), Christine and Jeff Doty, Cindy and Rodney Knier, Mary and Sarah Stover, and Lara Hughey. Friends like you are priceless.

Sunday Parfitt, for inspiring the first line with your parental wisdom.

Pastor Brian C. Johnson and the Kingdom Writers, for accountability and prayers.

Marianna Baer and Courtney Miller at Skyscape, for your expertise and enthusiasm.

And now, I'd like to thank my children even though I promised them I wouldn't, because they make fun of me every year for being somewhat crazy during National Novel Writing Month. So, Spencer, Ellen, Joel, and Matthias, this is me not thanking you. I love you anyway.

Most of all, I want to thank God. You made beauty from ashes, just as you promised you would.

ABOUT THE AUTHOR

Carrie Anne Noble is a former staff writer for a Pennsylvania newspaper. A member of Kingdom Writers and St. David's Christian Writers Association, she also eagerly participates in National Novel Writing Month each November and meets bimonthly with other NaNoWriMo writers in her area. Besides making stuff up, she enjoys reading, encouraging fellow writers, spending time with her family, and attempting to garden. *The Mermaid's Sister* is her first published novel.